EVA CHASE

CORRUPT ALCHEMY

ROYALS OF VILLAIN ACADEMY #5

Corrupt Alchemy

Book 5 in the Royals of Villain Academy series

All rights reserved. This book or any portion thereof may not be reproduced or used in any manner without the express written permission of the author, except for the use of brief quotations in a book review.

This is a work of fiction. Any resemblance to actual persons, living or dead, or actual events is purely coincidental.

First Digital Edition, 2019

Copyright © 2019 Eva Chase

Cover design: Fay Lane Cover Design

Ebook ISBN: 978-1-989096-50-5

Paperback ISBN: 978-1-989096-51-2

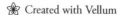 Created with Vellum

CHAPTER ONE

Rory

Since arriving at Bloodstone University, I'd been told a whole lot of things I'd found hard to believe—not least of all that I was the sole surviving member of one of the five ruling families of fear-based magic. I wouldn't have thought anything could surprise me at this point. But now I found myself tensed on the end of my bed, the warmth of the midday sun that streamed through my dorm-room window made suddenly distant by the thudding of my heart, unable to do anything but stare at Lillian Ravenguard as I struggled to process her last words.

"You think my mother is still alive," I repeated. The birth mother who'd supposedly died when I was two, seventeen years ago.

Lillian, who'd told me she'd been one of my mother's closest friends, looked as discomforted with the idea as I felt, though probably for different reasons.

"The small team of blacksuits who've been working on this with me haven't been able to confirm it for sure," she said. "In the past month, I've noticed a few subtle but unusual occurrences around possessions I have that she gave to me. The other day I took a tiny sample of your skin—I'm sorry for the subterfuge, but I didn't want to say anything until I had more concrete evidence to go by—and using that we were able to see a resonance in a seeking spell that suggested a genetic relative."

The other day? Oh, the day she'd come to see me here on campus, asking if *I'd* seen any unusual effects and brushing her fingers over my arm with a brief pinching that I'd wondered about afterward. I rubbed my wrist instinctively.

I didn't trust the woman in front of me, no matter how much a fixture she'd been in my family's life when I was too young to remember. She was high up in the blacksuits, the fearmancer law enforcement organization that had killed my adoptive parents in front of me this past spring and arrested me on a false murder charge just a couple weeks ago. A few *minutes* ago, my familiar had identified Lillian as the actual murderer of my friend and roommate, Imogen.

But I couldn't see why the woman would lie about this, especially in private. I had enemies high up in the fearmancer community who wanted to crush my spirit and get me under their control, and she appeared to have allied herself with them, but nothing about her suggestion or the way she was acting felt like it played into one of those schemes.

Of course, there were plenty of other reasons to question the idea.

"I've seen the report on the attack where I was kidnapped," I said. "There are photos of the bodies—my mother's and my father's—"

"I know," Lillian said, her gaze dropping to her hands. "I took part in the investigation. That's behind some of my hesitation to share this possibility with anyone, including you. My best guess would be that the body we took to be your mother's was a conjured replica. It was burned so badly we couldn't definitively identify it as her, but everyone else who'd been in the building was accounted for, and the basic details matched up…"

"Who would have made the replica?" I asked. "You think the *joymancers* did that during the attack?"

"Given the other information we have, that's the only conclusion that makes sense." Lillian swiped a hand across her mouth. It didn't dislodge her frown. "They took her prisoner at the same time as they kidnapped you, and they conjured the replica so we wouldn't come looking for her. Maybe they meant to do the same for you, but our forces got to the scene too quickly. I'm not sure."

"And then the joymancers, what, took her away to some prison?" It was hard to wrap my head around that idea. My mother had been the most powerful person in the building at the time of the attack—possibly the most powerful person in the entire fearmancer world. The Bloodstones were considered the highest family among the barons. It'd have been hard enough for anyone to overpower her. To risk taking her prisoner…

True, I'd learned enough about joymancers in the last few months that I no longer assumed they had to have good intentions. The mages who got their power from provoking joy in people could be just as vicious as those who got power from fear. But even without assuming good intentions, what would be the point in capturing one of the fearmancer barons and holding her captive for years on end?

They'd shown no qualms about killing the other fearmancers who'd been there during the attack. What would they have wanted her alive for?

"That's the only plausible possibility," Lillian said. "That is, if she *is* alive and the signs haven't misled us. They must have her locked away somewhere with her magic so tightly contained that it's taken her all these years to find a way to reach out to us at all, and then only faintly."

I wasn't sure if that made the situation better or worse. The joymancers hadn't slaughtered my mother like they had my father. They'd only shut her away for nearly two decades with no access to friends and family? Separating her from me, her child who'd been only a toddler when all this had happened? That was pretty sadistic torture right there.

Had she known that *I'd* survived the attack and was being raised by joymancers, or had she been told that I was dead like everyone had believed she was? Both of those options sounded pretty torturous too.

A pang of homesickness ran through me, familiar even if the sensation had been rising up less often as I'd adjusted to my new life. Growing up, I hadn't realized I'd once had any other parents at all. I'd loved the joymancer couple I'd known as Mom and Dad, and I still believed they'd loved me too. And right now I couldn't help wishing I could turn to them and ask them what the hell I was supposed to do with this news.

Had *they* known my birth mother was alive the whole time? Oh God.

"So what happens next?" I asked, curling my fingers into the bedspread to hold back the urge to hug myself. That wouldn't look very dignified. "Why are you telling me now if you're still not sure?"

Who else had she told? Did the older barons, the heads of the ruling families who had full authority over the community, already know? What would they make of this news?

They were the ones who'd instigated most of the horrors I'd faced since arriving at the university. Would they *want* to see my mother returned to them after all that?

"We're still keeping this information confidential to select members of the blacksuits until we have definite confirmation," Lillian said, which I supposed mostly answered my silent questions. "But to get that confirmation, we could use your help, which is why I've come to you. A strong genetic tie, like child to parent, can make certain types of magic easier, especially if you're consciously participating. We'd first want to prove that the presence we've sensed is definitely your mother, and then narrow down her location."

"So you can bring her back the way you brought me," I filled in. My stomach twisted at the thought.

It'd been awful for the joymancers to treat my birth mother the way they had, but given how the top fearmancers treated even their own, I could imagine how the opposing mages might have seen it as justified. And the blacksuit version of a rescue operation had resulted in a lot of bloodshed in my case. Getting my mother out of whatever facility the joymancer Conclave had trapped her in would probably require getting *through* a hell of a lot more people, some of whom would have had no say in or might not even know what they were guarding.

"That's what we'd hope, naturally." Lillian exhaled slowly. "I know this is a lot for you to take in, Rory. I'm sorry I had to spring it on you like this, especially so soon after the ordeal you've just been through with the hearing. After seventeen years, I'd just like to see your mother home again as soon as we can reach her."

That was fair. Whatever happened after, I did need to know whether my birth mother was even truly out there.

"All right," I said. "Let me know how you need me to participate in those spells, and I'll do what I can."

I drew my back up a little straighter as I spoke, calling on the inner strength that had served me well over my time here at Blood U, which had been far from easy so far. The joymancers weren't completely off when they called the place Villain Academy. But I'd made allies here now; I'd come into my magic. I was the heir of Bloodstone, and if my mother was alive somewhere in the world, I wasn't going to leave her rotting away in a prison cell.

I just might have a few things to say about the exact method we used to get her out of that prison cell.

Lillian nodded approvingly. "We have a few preparations to make, and there's been a pattern to the times when we seem most likely to reach her presence. I'll call on you within the next couple days, with as much advance notice as I can give you. Your professors will understand if you need to miss a class or two on blacksuit business."

"Got it." I had a little time to absorb this development, then.

Lillian seemed to realize I needed that time. "Thank you for your help," she said, moving to the door. "I hope we'll have good news about your mother soon." Then she slipped out with barely a sound, leaving me alone.

Well, not entirely alone. As soon as I flopped back on the bed, my familiar came scurrying out from her hiding place to join me. Deborah nestled her small mouse body next to my arm.

I hesitated for a second before saying anything to her. She'd been with me for years, though I'd only discovered that we were magically connected—and that she could communicate with me like a person, if only telepathically—after the fearmancers had wrenched me from my home. But the human spirit that resided within the animal had been a joymancer in her original life, and Deborah had been resistant to any criticism of her former colleagues.

The Conclave had arranged for her to reside in the mouse, and for that mouse to be bound to me as my familiar, so that she could keep an eye on me and warn them if I started showing the magical abilities they'd meant to suppress. The magical abilities the joymancers had kept secret from me for my entire life, letting me believe I was just a Nary—a regular person with no supernatural abilities at all.

Deborah said her job was also to protect me… but the more I learned about the mages who'd stolen me away, the less sure I was that she was being entirely honest about that.

"You heard all that?" I said, keeping my voice low. The dorm's walls were thin. No one else here knew I had a joymancer's spirit inside my familiar—I might be arrested for treason if they found out.

My ears are pretty sharp, Deborah said, the dry voice of a woman who'd have been in her sixties trickling into my head. *After what that woman did to your friend, I'm not sure you can trust anything she says.*

"She admitted she wasn't sure whether the presence she's sensed really is my mother. It seems like a strange thing to lie about." I paused. "So you never heard anything about the joymancers keeping the Bloodstone baron prisoner?"

That's the sort of information the Conclave would have kept extremely restricted, I'd imagine. I didn't even know who you really were, you remember, only that you were a fearmancer of some sort. I certainly never encountered anything that would suggest the story is true.

"But that doesn't mean it isn't." Although if Deborah hadn't heard about it, probably my adoptive parents hadn't known either.

Just be wary, Lorelei. These people have never had your well-being in mind. Have you arranged for that illusion spell to be placed on your necklace? That might be useful as they begin these ceremonies, to make sure the results are real.

"Yes, I talked to my Illusion professor this morning." Professor Burnbuck had agreed to cast a spell that would let me distinguish an illusion from reality, at least across a certain number of uses until I drained the magic. "He said he should have it ready by tomorrow."

That's something, then. I'll keep my ears perked around the building as usual.

I glanced at the time and sat up with a groan. I had a seminar to get to in fifteen minutes, even if the last thing I wanted to do while all these thoughts were colliding in my head was perform for an audience. As I grabbed my bag, the questions kept battering me.

What would I do if my mother was as dead as we'd always believed and this was all some bizarre trick?

What would I do if it wasn't?

CHAPTER TWO

Rory

I did my best to appear alert and attentive during class, but apparently my acting skills weren't up to par. Connar Stormhurst fell into step beside me right as I left the room.

"Are you all right?" he asked as we headed down the stairs of Nightwood Tower, where nearly all of the university's classes were held. "Has anyone been hassling you today? You seemed like you were struggling a little."

I grimaced. "Was it that obvious?"

He tucked one of his brawny arms around my shoulders in a sideways hug. "Only because I know you pretty well."

He did, in more ways than one. Connar was one of my fellow scions, the heirs to the fearmancer baronies. When I'd first arrived at the school, he'd been the only one who'd ended up accepting me... until his loyalty to the other scions, who hadn't felt so friendly, had driven him to push me away. But he'd more than made up for that brief period of hostility, even though standing by my side meant standing against his vicious parents, who only saw me as an obstacle to their plans.

He'd defended me and supported me when I'd needed it, and just the brush of his fingertips over my arm sparked a flutter of desire low in my belly. My feelings for the Stormhurst scion definitely went beyond friendship, as did his for me.

There were just a couple problems with that fact. One was that over time, I'd found myself drawn to *all* of the four guys who were meant to rule alongside me one day. So far they'd been willing to accept that I wasn't ready to decide between them and even to share some of our intimate moments, maybe because of the second problem.

Thanks to my position as the only heir of Bloodstone, whoever I took as a permanent partner would automatically have to become a Bloodstone too, meaning they couldn't become baron for their own family. I couldn't imagine asking anyone to make that sacrifice. Even if my mother was alive and returned to take up the barony for now, at her age and with my father gone, it didn't seem likely she'd be having more kids.

For now, it didn't matter. For now, we were college students enjoying each other's company and forming bonds that would hopefully work to our benefit when we ruled together, and the rest we could worry about later.

"I found out something unexpected," I told Connar.

"Something big. Not necessarily *bad*, but… we should probably all talk about it together."

I didn't need to tell him that by "we" I meant the scions. He nodded, his arm sliding across my back so he could clasp my hand as we left the tower. And it turned out we didn't need to go far to start setting up that meeting, because the oldest of the scions, Declan Ashgrave, was already striding across the green between the main campus buildings to meet us.

The Ashgrave scion's expression looked typically pensive. Along with being the oldest, Declan was the closest of us to being full baron, since his mother had died in the same confrontation that had supposedly claimed both of my parents' lives. He'd been sitting with the older barons in their pentacle for years now and would be considered a full member when he finished his schooling in a few months—and he took the responsibilities of that position very seriously, especially since he didn't agree with a lot of the older barons' attitudes.

Up until just this morning, Declan had also been employed by the school as a teacher's aide, which had meant consorting with the students could get him into major trouble. We hadn't been all that great at sticking to that rule, as much as he'd tried to keep our relationship strictly professional. But he'd resigned from his position today. We hadn't had the chance to talk yet about what that would mean for our relationship.

It didn't look like we'd be talking about it now either. When he stopped in front of us, his face stayed tensed, his bright hazel eyes dimmed with concern. "I don't suppose either of you has heard anything from Malcolm since the hearing?"

My heart skipped a beat. Of the scions, my association with Malcolm Nightwood had been the most fraught. He'd spent the first few months I'd attended the school trying to crush me into submission—because I openly disapproved of how harsh he was on the junior students, because I'd still been loyal to the joymancers who'd raised me, and various other justifications.

After a particular intense encounter between us, he'd backed off and even started helping me out here and there. I'd gotten a chance to see his better qualities and to understand why he'd resented me. And there was a spark of attraction between us that I hadn't been able to deny even when I'd been horrified by it.

Just a few days ago, he'd confessed to me that he "adored" me, that he'd wanted us to make a go of being together. I'd been tempted, even if I hadn't been sure I could totally trust him. Then yesterday at the hearing, he'd unexpectedly stepped up to testify on my behalf while his father, who'd wanted nothing more than to see me fall, looked on... I'd never expected Malcolm to throw in his lot with me that blatantly. It wasn't hard to imagine there'd been some fallout from his decision.

"I haven't," I said as Connar shook his head. "Why?"

"He hasn't been back on campus since the hearing," Declan said. "He missed a class this morning... One of the Nightwood employees brought his car around to the school garage yesterday, so he didn't go anywhere in that.

After the way he went against his father yesterday, I don't like it."

Connar's mouth slanted at a grim angle. My chest tightened. "Do you think his dad would have *hurt* him somehow in punishment?"

I didn't know much about Baron Nightwood other than he was incredibly intimidating and didn't take well to being disobeyed. But Connar had told me horrible stories about how his own parents had forced him and his brother to attack each other, and indicated he thought Malcolm's family was even more brutal. If his father had retaliated, I didn't think it'd be a simple grounding.

And whatever had happened to him, it'd been because of what Malcolm had done for me. I might not be walking free at all if not for him. If he hadn't said what he had, I wasn't sure the witness who'd been able to clear my name would have had the courage to speak up as well.

"I don't know." Declan frowned as he glanced toward Ashgrave Hall, which held the senior dorms, the library, and, in the basement, the private scion lounge room. "Jude's in the lounge—he hasn't heard from Malcolm either. Why don't we join him and sort out between the four of us what we want to do about it?"

"Rory had something she needed to tell us about too," Connar put in.

Declan's gaze shot to me with even more worry than before. I held up my hands. "It's important, but not quite as immediate as this thing with Malcolm. We can tackle one subject at a time."

We crossed the green to the old stone building and

slipped past the library to the stairwell that led to the lounge. When we came into the wide, brightly lit room with its entertainment system, pool table, and bar cabinet, Jude Killbrook was standing near the TV, poking through the video game cases stacked there. At our entrance, he straightened up in an instant, swiping his floppy dark copper hair back from his eyes. A brilliant smile flashed across his face when his eyes met mine.

The Killbrook scion hadn't exactly been welcoming when I'd first arrived, but he'd warmed up to me a lot faster than Malcolm had. I'd become more appealing as a friend and ally when he'd realized I wouldn't judge him for the dangerous secret he'd been carrying. Jude *wasn't* actually the heir of the Killbrook family—he wasn't a Killbrook at all. When his parents hadn't been able to conceive on their own, his father had gotten paranoid that his position as baron would be challenged and had arranged for Jude's mother to get pregnant by another man under magical coercion.

From what I'd heard, Baron Killbrook had never been able to come to terms with the scheme he'd set in motion himself. He'd shunned Jude from childhood. And now the Killbrooks were finally expecting a child that was really their own. Once a "real" heir existed, the old one was a liability, his mere existence making him a threat capable of exposing his father's treachery.

I was the only one on campus who Jude had dared to tell. He was very good at hiding any uncomfortable emotions under a mask of joking nonchalance.

"Are we assembling a rescue mission, then?" he said to Declan with a teasing arch of his eyebrows.

"I don't know if I'd go quite that far," Declan said. "But we might want to do something."

He sat down on one of the armchairs while I ended up on the couch between Connar and Jude. Connar's hand stayed twined with mine, and Jude's came to rest on my knee with an affectionate squeeze. If seeing their comfortable intimacy with me bothered Declan after we'd had to suppress our feelings for each other for so long, he didn't show it. Of course, spending time with the older barons, he'd had to get good at hiding his emotions too.

"Has Malcolm ever disappeared like this before?" I asked.

Declan shook his head. "As far as I can remember, he's never missed a class unless it was on some kind of official business that we all knew about. It's important to him to grow his skills as much as possible and to set an example for the other students."

"Yeah," Connar said. "And even if he *hadn't* had classes today, if he was going to take off on some kind of trip, he'd usually give us a heads up so we'd know where he is if we need him." He pulled out his phone. "I can try texting him."

"Give it a shot," Declan said. "I did earlier, and he hasn't replied. Batteries can die or he could be somewhere he couldn't bring his phone, but on top of everything else…"

My free hand rose to my chest with the urge to fidget with my necklace—the one Professor Burnbuck had right now. "What exactly do you all think his family would do to him?"

"When it comes to Baron Nightwood? Who knows?" Jude muttered. "My dad is fucking terrified of him."

Declan made a face. "It's hard to say. Malcolm's never gone against him even in small ways that I'm aware of. The Nightwoods could be pretty harsh simply over a mistake or expectations not quite met." He hesitated. "I don't know if the rest of you ever noticed the little bruises and other minor injuries—Malcolm's always been pretty careful about covering them up."

My chest clenched with the memory of a day a few months ago when I'd stumbled on Malcolm at a time he'd thought he was alone. I'd seen a burn mark on the back of his shoulder in the few seconds before he'd noticed I was here—he'd gotten awfully defensive about it when I'd asked if he was okay. Had his father done that to him, purposefully?

Had his father done that a *lot*?

Jude's mouth had tightened. "You're the Insight man, so you'd pick up more than we would. But yeah, there've been a few times I caught a hint of an illusion on him and saw it slip a bit…"

Connar looked horrified. He'd told me Malcolm was the scion he'd considered his closest friend, the one who'd stood by him without any judgment. "After what he did at the hearing… his dad would come down on him a hundred times worse, wouldn't he?"

I swallowed hard. What he'd done at the hearing had

been all for me. Malcolm must have known punishment would come, too.

Why hadn't I insisted he come with the rest of us when we'd left the hearing? I'd been so worn out from the stress leading up to it and overwhelmed by relief. Fuck.

"That's why I think it might be a good idea to check on him," Declan said. "I'm assuming he's at the main Nightwood residence in Connecticut. It's only a couple hours' drive. I can't imagine we have to worry about whether he's *alive*, considering how long his father has been grooming him as heir, but if he doesn't turn up soon, we could at least make sure he is there and see if there's anything we can do to help. He'd do the same for any of us."

"Yes, he would." Connar stood up. "Why don't we go *now*?"

"Baron Nightwood isn't going to be pleased about the bunch of us showing up on his doorstep demanding access," Jude pointed out.

"And at this point, by the time we got out there, it'd be the end of the day." Declan motioned vaguely toward the door. "His parents will probably be home. If it's bad, they won't want us to talk to him. And maybe it's not that serious and he'll be back tonight. I think, given the present tensions within the pentacle of barons and between us and them, it's best if we take a careful approach, or we could bring even more anger down on him."

Connar sank back down. "That's true."

"I know his dad has appointments tomorrow," Declan went on. "I'll be the least conspicuous coming by since I have professional connections to both Nightwoods. I thought I'd drive out with one of you, and I'll distract the staff while whoever's with me sneaks off to find and talk to Malcolm. Any of us has enough magical ability to avoid the household employees."

"I'll go with you," I said before anyone else had a chance to speak. When both Jude and Connar turned to blink at me, I barreled on. "If his dad has messed him up, it's because Malcolm stood up for me. I owe him for that. And my only class tomorrow is late in the afternoon, so it won't be obvious to anyone around here that I took off for the day as long as we're back on time."

If taking my side had cost Malcolm badly, I should have to face that. I should offer him whatever I could to help him through.

"Are you sure?" Jude said. "If his dad finds out *you* came sneaking around his property…"

I shrugged. "Baron Nightwood already hates me and wants me stripped of my magic. I don't think he can get any more hostile than he's already been."

"All right," Declan said. "Let's consider it settled. Meet me at the garage at nine, and we should be able to get back from the trip with plenty of time to spare." He studied me. "What was it you wanted to talk to us about?"

For a little while, I'd almost forgotten my conversation with Lillian. Now it rushed back to me with stomach-knotting vividness.

I wet my lips. "Well, there's two things. The blacksuit who's reached out to me as a family friend, Lillian Ravenguard? I'm pretty sure she's the one who killed

Imogen." I couldn't tell them I was completely sure without revealing that I knew from Deborah—and how far from just a mouse Deborah was.

Connar sucked in a rough breath. I held up my hand. "That's not the biggest news. She came to talk to me today because she thinks… there's a chance my mother might still be alive and in joymancer custody."

Jude's jaw dropped. "What the hell?"

"That was my first response too," I said with a weak smile, and repeated what Lillian had been able to tell me. "So it's not definite," I finished. "I'll let you know whether they're able to confirm anything after they do these ceremonies. I don't even know what to think—what would happen with, well, *everything* if she came back."

Silence hung over the four of us for a moment. We'd just finished talking about how cruel fearmancer parents, especially barons, could be. I had no idea what kind of mother Baron Bloodstone would have shown herself as if she'd had me in her life for more than two years. I had no idea how she'd fit in with the other barons after all this time or how she'd respond to the way they'd turned on me.

"It would shake up the pentacle, that much we could count on," Declan said. "Exactly how… We can't know until we come to that. I suppose all you can do is take it one step at a time and see."

"Yeah," I said quietly. And hope that whatever upheaval followed, it'd shake up in my favor rather than against me.

CHAPTER THREE

Jude

I turned the glass charm over in my hand, murmuring a casting word here and there to test the spell bound through its shape. The magic Professor Burnbuck had imbued the material with involved several complex strands, not all of which I could have wound together myself, but nothing that set off any concerns.

I gave the charm another onceover just to be safe, because it was Rory's security I was evaluating here, and then handed the necklace back to its owner. "I don't sense any hostile or harmful spells, or anything that would activate an illusion of its own. As far as I can tell, it'll do exactly what the professor said it would."

Rory sighed in relief where she was sitting next to me on the steps outside Killbrook Hall and fastened the necklace around her neck. "Good. I didn't *want* to think he'd try to screw me over too, but the way things have been going…"

"Yeah. I fully approve of your instinct for caution."

She smiled and leaned into me, and I happily slipped my arm around her waist to complete the embrace. When I turned to kiss the top of her head, the sweet smell of her hair filled my nose. We'd met early enough in the morning that only a few students were meandering around the university grounds, not that I cared who saw us anyway. I couldn't really have made my interest in the Bloodstone scion any clearer over the last few months.

The sky overhead was brilliant blue except for a few streaks of cloud, but the coolness in the breeze said fall was basically here, even if the calendar didn't agree quite yet. The trees in the forest that separated campus from the nearby town hadn't started changing color yet, but I could practically taste the shift in the air. That was my favorite time of year here: when the leaves turned into a riot of vividness that even an illusionist would find it difficult to top.

"I have to go meet Declan soon," Rory said without moving.

"I know. I'm going to enjoy your company for the little time I have with you this morning."

I stroked my fingers over her hair, and she raised her head, and then there really wasn't anything I could do except kiss her. My fingers dropped to her cheek. Her mouth met mine, warm and soft and so eagerly that for a moment I wished I could just drown in her. Why did anything in the world have to matter other than this girl?

But that kind of thinking wasn't going to help me now that I was basically on my own. Turning Rory into some kind of hedonistic escape wasn't what she deserved either. I'd spent most of my first year here on campus drowning myself in alcohol to try to numb myself to the constant reminders of what a fraud I was, and that hadn't led anywhere good. I wasn't going to turn the only girl I'd ever loved into a vice.

Even though I'd have liked to at least keep kissing her, I drew back after I'd sated the most immediate urge, because I had important things I hadn't said yet.

"You'll be careful out there?" I said, keeping my hand against her cheek. "I know Declan's sure that the old man won't be around, but if Baron Nightwood thinks he can take a strike at you on his own property with no one nearby to witness it…"

I was a little worried about Malcolm and his unusual absence too, of course, but he'd known what he was getting into when he'd gone against his dad. Rory couldn't, not really. Even after everything she'd seen, everything the barons and their allies had done to her, I didn't think she could fully comprehend how far someone like Baron Nightwood might go to get his way.

"I'm not going to be taking any unnecessary risks," she said. "*I* don't want to have to face Malcolm's dad any more than you'd want that to happen. I'll go straight to Malcolm's room, look around a little more if I can't find him there, and then get back out again. Quick and simple."

She mentioned Malcolm's name calmly enough, but

I'd seen her face when we'd been talking about what he might have endured at his father's hands yesterday. I'd seen the way they'd looked at each other a few days ago when I'd interrupted their conversation in the scion lounge. In between the glowers and the verbal challenges, there'd been a hell of a lot of heat, and not generated by the anger it might have been due to just last term.

I was hardly surprised to see sparks fly. Malcolm had made *his* interest in Rory clear in the first few weeks she'd been on campus. And now that he'd gotten his head out of his ass and started treating her with the respect and consideration she deserved, why shouldn't she soften to him too? Even if she was starting to see him as some kind of prospect, she'd told him in no uncertain terms that she wasn't going to break things off with me to appease him— and then minutes later shown him just how little she'd let him order her around in a statement I'd very much enjoyed.

So I shouldn't have been worried about it. I'd already accepted that she had something going with Connar too. She wasn't like any fearmancer girl any of us had ever encountered—how could she be, with the way she'd been raised? So, why wouldn't she bring out something powerful in all of us?

All the same, some part of me insisted on dredging up the subject.

"So, you and Malcolm have… sorted out your differences?" I ventured.

Rory cocked her head at me, obviously reading a whole lot of what I'd restrained myself from saying just from my tone. She smiled crookedly. "I'm not completely sure what's happening there. There's been a lot to sort out after everything he put me through, and dealing with the hearing at the same time... But I meant what I said to him. Maybe he and I can get to the point where we have something like I have with you, but not if he tries to insist I can't be with anyone else. I'm not throwing what we have away."

She grasped my hand as she said those last words as if to emphasize her point. My heart squeezed in a way I wasn't totally comfortable with yet but still welcomed. I believed her. It was only my stupid insecurities about who I was and what I was supposed to be that provoked any doubts.

"I got an apartment in Manhattan," I said abruptly, without knowing I was going to mention it before the words spilled out. "I didn't want to have to go back to the Killbrook residence when school's on break. Maybe this weekend, I could have you over to see it?"

A much more definite smile crossed Rory's face then. "I'd love to. And that sounds like a really good step for you to take. How did your father react?"

"I didn't talk to him about it. He hasn't gotten in touch. As far as I know, he's just glad to have me out of his hair."

I didn't really think I could count on my separation from the family being that simple, but there was no point in worrying Rory about things that hadn't happened yet.

"I'm taking precautions to make sure the apartment is secure," I added, in case she would anyway.

"Good. I'm looking forward to seeing the place. I'm sure it'll be a nice change from gloomy stone mansions." She laughed a little and stood up—time for her to go.

I tugged her to me for one more kiss, channeling my rush of happiness into the gesture. Then I dipped my head by her ear. "I love you," I said—softly, but it got easier each time I formed the words.

Rory gave me another quick kiss, her eyes shining as she gazed back at me. "I love you too."

And then she was loping across the parking lot toward the garage, where she was going to drive off to see another guy she might also be falling in love with. I just had to not be jealous about that.

In some ways, my disadvantage was also my advantage, I reminded myself. I was the only one of the scions who could make a permanent commitment to her without losing my position, because it wasn't actually my position to begin with. A mixed blessing.

I'd meant to go back to my dorm room to finish up my paper for World Economics, but as I circumnavigated the hall that bore my family's name, a flicker of movement at the corner of my eye caught my attention.

I paused on the edge of the green and took a slow scan around with as casual an air as I could put on, as if I were lost in thought and my gaze simply meandering. At the same time, I spoke a quick word under my breath. A wisp of the magic gathered at the base of my throat tingled up to my eyes.

There. Standing by the corner of Killbrook Hall, a figure blinked into view when I kept my eyes aimed just a little away from it. A man, middle-aged as far as I could tell without looking at him directly, wearing nondescript clothes that could easily have blended in with the maintenance staff. Except for some reason he had an illusion cast over him to help him also blend into the stone wall behind him. That didn't bode well.

I waited for a minute to see if he'd follow Rory to the garage, but he didn't show any sign of even looking in her direction. No, he appeared to be watching *me*. An uneasy prickling ran over my skin.

It was an easy enough theory to test. I set off across the green, toward the lake rather than the residences to put more distance between us. Halfway along the path, I veered off to the side toward the kennel where Malcolm's familiar lived. Connar had planned on giving the wolf a run and a chance to hunt yesterday after we'd determined that Malcolm was missing, but the animal was probably getting stir-crazy again. I could probably get away with letting it out for a bit even though class time had technically started.

And this gave me the opportunity to judge whether I was being followed.

In the middle of the field, I stopped as if I'd seen something in the grass and bent down. As I reached for the ground, I glanced around surreptitiously, murmuring my casting word to deflect illusions again.

The guy *had* followed me. He was more visible now that he'd had to move away from his original post—it was always harder to keep up camouflaging illusions when in motion. He'd come around Ashgrave Hall and stopped there near the building, his face still turned in my direction.

Well, my instincts had been set off by more than paranoia, clearly. This jackass was tailing me. I didn't know why, but I could make a solid guess.

I'd just removed myself from my supposed father's domain and aligned myself in every possible way with the soon-to-be baron he saw as a threat. Now he was having people keep an eye on me to see what I'd do next.

Or to make sure I couldn't do anything at all.

My mouth went dry. I debated the merits of marching right up to the guy and telling him off, but that'd just mean the next people my father sent would take even more care to disguise their surveillance. And maybe it'd make Dad think I needed a firmer hand than he'd taken in this situation so far.

No, for now it was better to lay low and stay sharp. While his people observed me, I could observe them right back—and make sure I didn't give away anything he could use against me or the other scions.

CHAPTER FOUR

Rory

It was so very Declan that while the other scions owned flashy, posh-looking cars—even *I* had a Lexus, courtesy of my inheritance—he drove a modest sedan, the kind no one would have looked twice at on the road or in a parking lot. It was also very him that the inside was perfectly neat, not a bit of litter on the floor or the dashboard.

He set a travel mug of coffee in the cup holder as I sank into the leather seat on the passenger side, which honestly, was just as comfortable as any fancier car I'd ever been in. The cedar scent I associated with him washed over me. I tipped my head back with a slow exhale. He hadn't even started the engine, and the thought of what we might find at the Nightwood mansion was already making me tense.

"I guess we don't have to worry so much about being

seen hanging out together now, huh?" I said. "Now that you're not a TA anymore?"

Declan ran his hand over his hair, smoothing the black strands he kept swept back from his forehead, before turning the key. The rumble of the engine hummed through the seats. "No one can accuse me of anything other than spending time with a colleague and friend," he said. "And that should hardly raise any eyebrows."

"Has there still been no sign of my grandparents?" My birth father's parents had come sniffing around trying to benefit from my return to the fearmancer world not that long ago—and they'd caught Declan and me in what we'd thought was a private moment. They hadn't seen clear proof that we were romantically involved, but it'd been enough for them to try to blackmail him and hassle me about it... until I'd given him the go-ahead to dig up a past crime of theirs for the blacksuits to pursue.

"They're still hiding out wherever they fled to in Europe," he said. "I don't think the blacksuits are trying all that hard to find them. Out of sight, out of mind. Even if they do come back and make a fuss, they don't have any evidence, and nothing we do from here on breaks any rules."

That was certainly a relief, but something about the way he'd talked about it niggled at me. I tried to put that discomfort into words as he drove the car out of the university garage and turned onto the road that led through town. Before I could, he changed the subject.

"Have you come up with a strategy for getting to Malcolm's room?"

Thinking about that concrete plan steadied me. "You said it's on the second floor around the side," I said. "So whoever you're talking to at the front door won't be able to keep an eye on it from the outside. I figured I'd use a similar trick to when I dropped in on your dorm room."

A couple months ago when I'd needed to speak to Declan in secret, I'd cast an illusion over the wall beneath my bedroom window and climbed down a rope to Declan's, which was right under mine. It'd worked well enough.

Declan let out a chuckle. "I guess there's something to be said for tried and true. You'd be going up instead of down this time, though. How are you going to fix the rope in place?"

"I'm conjuring it, so I figure I can meld it with the window frame. Assuming the window's open. I guess if it's not I can use a spell to handle that too." I frowned, trying to picture the possibilities. "It seems a lot less likely I'd get caught if I go straight from the outside rather than navigating the entire house, anyway."

"Fair enough. If he's in there, I suppose he'll get an interesting surprise."

I tapped Declan lightly with my elbow. "Maybe I should pay you a surprise visit again some night now that we don't have to worry so much."

When he didn't immediately respond to my teasing flirtation, my stomach dropped. "I mean, if you'd like that. I don't know—we never did get to talk—" *That* was what had bothered me. The uncertainty, the way he'd talked about me as a "colleague and friend" when I couldn't help seeing him as so much more.

Connar might have been the first of the scions to show me much friendliness, but Declan had never been cruel. He'd just been trying to keep his distance to protect himself and his family. But even with those responsibilities hanging over him and all the pressures he was facing from the barons, who'd wanted him to help them get me in line, he'd done more to look out for me than anyone else at Blood U had. He'd taught me how to shield my mind, he'd helped me understand both the community I belonged to and the one I'd thought I did, he'd investigated his other colleagues, and he'd even gotten me out of the blacksuits' prison and ensured I had all the time I needed to defend myself.

And the few times he'd given in to the attraction that sizzled between us, he'd shown me a mix of passion and tenderness that lit a flame in my core just remembering it.

I wanted more of that. I'd hoped he did too. He'd hinted that it was at least part of the reason he'd resigned as a teacher's aide. But he'd had a little more time to think about it now. He'd struggled with the fact that he couldn't ever make a real commitment to me without giving up the Ashgrave barony and placing all the responsibilities—and danger—that came with it on his younger brother's shoulders. Maybe he'd decided that having me and then giving me up would be too painful after all.

"Rory," Declan said, so gently that my most immediate worries faded. "I'm sorry. I wasn't sure if it was a good time to get into all that with this news about your mother and the concerns about Malcolm and everything. We can talk about it now if you'd like. We do have a couple hours on the road ahead of us."

"Yeah," I said, my heart beating a little faster. "I think that would be good. Just so I know where we stand. What's okay and what's not. Maybe there aren't any rules to worry about now, but I still don't want to put you in an uncomfortable position."

"I don't think that's very likely. I—" He cut himself off for a moment, his gaze fixed on the road ahead, his hands flexing where they gripped the steering wheel. "The thing I realized is that the steps I told myself I was taking to spare myself pain… They didn't really make sense. I was *already* in pain staying away from you."

He glanced over at me, his hazel eyes so intent I couldn't have looked away if I'd wanted to. "I love you, Rory. I've been falling for you since you first stood up to Malcolm and refused to take his shit, and every time we talk, every stand I watch you take, I just fall harder."

A hot flush spread up my neck and over my cheeks. The emotion in my chest swelled up so fast it clogged my throat. I couldn't say more than, "Declan…"

He had to draw his gaze back to the road, but he kept talking. "It's been *killing* me holding myself back from saying any of that, from showing any of it… Seeing Jude and Connar be there for you in all the ways I've wanted to be… What does it matter if we know it can only be temporary? We could have *years* of temporary before we have to focus on settling down and making our own families. I'd rather enjoy whatever moments we can have together and deal with the pain when it's time to end it than only have the painful parts."

"Yeah." I swallowed hard. "I see it the same way. Declan, I love you too."

A hint of a flush colored his own face. "That's a relief. Then I don't have to feel like a total idiot for confessing it."

"There wouldn't have been anything idiotic about saying it even if I wasn't ready to say it back." I looked down at my hands. "If anything, I feel like there's something wrong with me. I can say that to you, and I've said it to Jude… and I think I love Connar too."

"But not Malcolm?" Declan said with a hint of a grin.

I let out an exasperated sound. "I'm still wrapping my head around the idea that I could *like* Malcolm. But, God, who knows? At this point, I probably shouldn't make any assumptions."

"As hard as I know it may be for you to believe, he can be charming when he wants to be. I've seen it with my own eyes."

"But this isn't how it's supposed to work, is it? Aren't people supposed to fall for one person at a time? I feel so greedy wanting all of you."

He shrugged. "You're figuring out who you really are, how you fit into this world, what you're capable of… I don't think it's that strange. We all have the choice of how far we go down that path with you and how we handle ourselves and our emotions. You've been honest with me the whole time about how you're feeling and what you're feeling for the other guys too. That's all I'd ask of you."

"You know, I only ever had one boyfriend my entire

life before this," I felt the need to say. "I wasn't some crazed nymphomaniac back in California."

Declan shot me an amused glance. "You don't strike me as all that crazed now, either."

I felt a little crazed when he looked at me like that, still a little pink from his confession and my returning it, full of fondness and desire. Why did we have to be talking about this while he was driving, when I couldn't even kiss him?

I waved my hand dismissively. "My point is just, I wasn't expecting this. So I'm doing my best."

"And your best is pretty damn good."

Okay, now I *really* wanted to kiss him. I settled for giving his shoulder a quick squeeze. I wasn't going to be responsible for a car accident in a moment of distraction.

Declan took one hand off the wheel just long enough to brush his fingers over mine. "I look forward to a less restricted new normal with you." He paused. "I do think we should avoid any especially overt public displays of affection and the like. We can be open about being friendly and spending time together, but I'm not sure how the other barons would react to us being romantically involved as well. It'd be easier not to have to deal with that if we don't have to."

I couldn't argue that. "I'm not sure I'd even want to deal with the reactions we'd get on campus if it was obvious I was dating all three of you. And I don't want to bring any more trouble down on you than you've already had to face for helping me. If that lets you toe the line with the pentacle of barons more easily, I'm happy to keep all our private activities… well, private."

"Then we're on exactly the same page," Declan said with a smile so pleased and warm it sent a tingle through me.

We drove on in a comfortable silence for a few minutes before he added, "You know, I'm glad you're reaching some kind of understanding with Malcolm, however that develops. He was harder on you than he should have been, and some of the tactics he used—he crossed some lines. But he isn't his father. He's still got a sense of honor and loyalty, which Baron Nightwood seems to have lost somewhere along the way. I think, with us all working together, that's the best way we can make sure *our* pentacle is a better one than theirs."

"Yeah," I said. "I'm starting to think ruling next to him might not be such a bad thing."

If I got to rule at all. I'd thought that in just a couple years, when Declan and I were both full barons, we could start pushing for change already. If my birth mother returned…

I pushed that thought out of my mind and focused on the road ahead. Lillian might be wrong. My mother might not even be alive. If she was, she might not *want* to deal with the stress of ruling anymore after all those years imprisoned. There was no way to know yet.

And I had a whole lot of more urgent things to worry about as we sped along the road toward Malcolm's family home.

CHAPTER FIVE

Rory

When Declan pulled the car onto the shoulder of the road, I knew we'd almost reached the Nightwood property. Time to get down to business.

"I'm going to cast two spells," he reminded me. "One so no one who looks at the car will see you through the window, and one to help disguise you while you're heading to the house. You'll still have to be cautious getting out of the car. I'll have some of the staff distracted inside. You'll probably want to cast a searching spell on the nearby windows to make sure no one's watching."

"Got it," I said. "And I'll want to get to the wall and cast my illusion there as quickly as possible to completely hide myself."

"Right. What I'm going to cast on you is more of a reflective effect to help you blend in with your current surroundings. It should work okay on the lawn where it's mostly grass, but it's still possible for someone to pick up on the effect if they're looking closely or have a lot of experience with illusions."

I nodded. My pulse was skittering in anticipation. After Jude's warning this morning, I couldn't help adding, "What if Baron Nightwood changed his schedule, and *he's* there after all?"

Declan gave me a firm look. "I wouldn't let you walk into a situation like that. I made a call to one of the people he's meeting with today and was able to confirm they're still expecting him. And I'll use insight on the staff to make sure there's nothing to worry about when I first talk to them. When you see me go inside, you can assume it's all clear."

"Okay." I kept my breaths even as Declan built the illusion on the windows and then on me with softly spoken words and subtle movements of his hands. He sat back and laughed roughly, looking at me with a twitch of his eyes.

"I can hardly focus on you now. At least that means I must have done my job well."

"You better have," I said, but my heart wasn't in the teasing.

It was only another minute's drive before the stone mansion came into view, looming as large as the Bloodstone fortress behind a gate that must have been twice my height. Declan leaned out his window and identified himself as "Baron Ashgrave" to the security camera. After a moment, the gate creaked open. That sound wasn't ominous at all.

We didn't speak as he came up the front drive to the house. The flutter of a curtain on one of the upper front windows made my nerves jitter all over again. I drew the casting I was planning into the back of my mouth with a quiver of the magic behind my collarbone.

Declan parked at the far north side of the circular drive, where I could make almost a straight run for the northern side of the house. I couldn't see the windows there yet, but I'd rehearsed his instructions in my head dozens of times. Second floor, far corner.

He reached over in a discreet motion to briefly grasp my hand. I took as much comfort from the contact as I could before he got out of the car.

Declan strode up to the mansion's front door and knocked. An employee opened it a moment later, probably already waiting for him. The entrance was far enough away from our parking spot that I couldn't make out anything either of them said, but Declan kept up a friendly smile and made a few casual gestures. After a few exchanges, the woman who'd answered the door stepped back, and he went into the front hall.

The door closed behind him. My heart stuttered. That was my cue.

I whispered my casting, peering at each of the windows I could see. None of them offered the tremble of energy that indicated a living presence nearby. Whoever had been peeking out before must have moved on at

Declan's entrance. All right then. I had to trust that he was keeping the closest staff occupied.

I pushed the car door open as gently as I could and eased it shut behind me, not quite closing it to ensure it didn't make a thud. Then I darted across the lawn around the side of the building.

A narrow bed of flowers lay along the north wall, just starting to wilt with the coming autumn. They gave off a sharp, slightly sour smell. As I headed for the far corner of the mansion, I kept my distance from the flowerbeds for as long as I could, since I didn't know how well Declan's reflective illusion would hold up against more complicated visuals.

The window at the end of the second floor was halfway open—enough of a gap that I'd be able to crawl through. That was one small relief. The other bit of luck was the thick stone ledge that protruded a few inches out from the wall. I'd fix my conjured rope to that.

Murmuring the words as quickly as I could while still focusing on the spell, I drew an illusion into place a couple feet in front of the wall. It recreated the wall's seams and dimples as closely as I could. By the time that was in place, sweat had broken out on my forehead and my pulse was thudding from more than just nerves. I squared my shoulders and summoned even more energy to create my rope.

I extended the narrow cord only to waist height, since my illusion didn't cover the flowerbed below that. Once my conjuring was complete, I could only allow myself a second to let out my breath before I hurried over and grasped the rope. The sooner I was out of sight behind my illusion, the better.

I'd modeled the rope after the real one I'd used to climb down to Declan's dorm room. It bit into my palms with its solid texture, but at least the coarseness stopped my hands from slipping. Going up two floors was definitely harder than going down one.

With my feet planted against the wall, I pulled myself upward one hand and step at a time. The muscles in my shoulders and back strained, but I made it up to the window in a matter of minutes. I grasped the inner lip of the ledge and hauled myself over it into the room.

I managed to catch myself before I tumbled all the way to the floor. My feet landed on the smooth hardwood with only a faint tap. Then I was standing in a dim room nearly as large as my dorm's common room back at Blood U. The only light was what seeped through the window. Despite the dimness, the space smelled fresh enough, with a hint of the aquatic tang I'd caught on Malcolm's skin before.

In the first second while I took in the space, I thought we'd made the wrong gamble—that he wasn't here and maybe not in the house at all. Nothing stirred by the big rolltop desk or the circle of armchairs around the fireplace near me, or by the massive four-poster bed at the far end of the room.

Then a voice emerged from what I'd taken for just a heap of covers, a little hoarse but undeniably Malcolm's demanding tone. "Hello?"

There was definitely a question in that word too. Couldn't he see it was me?

I wouldn't have expected to find him in bed this late in the morning. He hadn't even bothered to sit up.

I hesitated and then walked over, tense and uncertain of my welcome. It didn't seem entirely implausible that he might snap at me for interrupting his sleep-in.

As I came up on the bed, his form became clearer, his body sprawled rigidly straight on his side in the middle of the mattress. A light blanket covered him up to his shoulders, his head with its topping of short golden-brown curls facing the wall ahead of me. When I passed the bed's foot, his dark gaze found me. He sucked in a rasp of breath.

"Stop right there."

The command came out ragged but so firm my legs locked even though there'd been no persuasive magic in the words. I couldn't read Malcolm's shadowed expression. He looked almost... horrified?

"I'm sorry for coming in like this without any warning," I started, keeping my voice low. "We were worried about you—we—"

"*Stop.*" He dragged in another breath. "When I scared you in the boathouse, what did you threaten to do to me?"

Why the hell was he bringing *that* up at this moment? I stared at him for a second before I found the words. "I said if you touched me again I'd break every bone in your hands. But that's not—I was upset—What does that have to do with anything right now?"

He shifted just a fraction with a raw laugh. "It is

actually you. God, Rory, you do know how to surprise a guy, don't you?"

His first words took a moment to sink in. "You thought I might just be an illusion or something? Who would…" I trailed off as the obvious answers presented themselves.

"My dad," Malcolm said, confirming the first possibility that had popped into my head. "To test how I'd react. How loyal I still am. I'm kind of surprised he hasn't tried that yet, come to think of it." An edge had crept into his voice. He paused, and when he spoke again, he'd smoothed it out. "What exactly are you doing here, actual Rory?"

I came right up to the side of the bed, still feeling awkward. There was something odd about the way he was lying there so motionless—he'd hardly tipped his head to look at me better. A chill ran down my back.

"I was trying to tell you," I said. "We were worried. The guys noticed you hadn't come back to school—you weren't responding to their texts—and we knew your dad had to be pissed off about you testifying for me at the hearing. It seemed a little much for all four of us to turn up on your doorstep, so it's just Declan and me. He's distracting the staff while I check whether you're okay. *Are* you okay?" He definitely didn't look like he was.

"I'm touched by your concern," Malcolm said in a wry tone, but something in his expression softened as if he did appreciate the gesture even as he mocked it. "Did someone think to give Shadow a run? He'll need it by now."

Being apart from his familiar for this long would only

add to whatever other discomfort he was feeling. "Connar went to look after him. I'll let him out today when I get back. What about you?"

Malcolm made a dismissive sound. "I expected this. I'll be out of here in another day or two. You don't have to worry about me, Glinda."

I wasn't letting his "good witch" nickname distract *me* from the fact that he hadn't actually answered the question. "Don't bullshit me. I'm here now. I can see something's wrong. It doesn't make you look stronger to lie about it. What did he do to you?" The thought of all the ways his father could have hurt him brought an ache into my throat.

"Leave it," Malcolm said. "I'll be fine."

I folded my arms over my chest. "I think you should know by now how stubborn I can be. If you're *currently* fine, why don't you sit up so we can have a proper conversation?"

Malcolm was silent for a long moment. He closed his eyes. "Apparently you and my father have similar ideas about physical discipline. Although he didn't limit himself to my hands. From the way it feels if I try to move, I have the feeling he's fractured bones in just about every part of my body. So I don't move, and it's not so bad."

The chill turned into an icy flood of horror that filled me from chest to gut. "He did that to you—because of the hearing?" *Because of me.*

"I stepped out of line in a major way. It's very important to him to make sure I remember never to do it again." He managed a faint chuckle and looked at me again. "I pretended I was just doing what I thought was best for the barony. Lord only knows what he'd have put me through if I'd admitted I'd wanted you to get off so you can put him in his place someday."

For fuck's sake, was that supposed to make me feel better? What had his father put him through *before* now that he could laugh this off as if it were a normal punishment?

He'd known. He'd stepped up to the witness seat knowing a backlash like this was going to come... and he'd done it anyway.

I wavered on my feet, my hands opening and closing at my sides, and then sat down on the edge of the bed gingerly, careful not to rock the mattress. "I don't know much about healing, but—is there anything I can do to help? Or I could tell Declan, and he could figure out something... We can't just leave you here like this."

"Of course you can," Malcolm said matter-of-factly. "You think we all wouldn't be in even deeper shit if he found out you'd interfered? He'll bring a fearmancer doctor around in the next couple days to fuse all those fractures, and other than the memory, it'll be like it never happened. I'll be back at school by Monday, and you can go back to putting *me* in my place. I guess it's good practice."

Somehow the casual way he spoke about it made the whole situation worse. As if he didn't think I could really care that much how he was suffering on my behalf. A sudden heat welled behind my eyes, so fast I had to blink hard.

Malcolm's forehead furrowed. "Are you… *crying*?"

I swiped at my eyes. "You're basically being tortured in the most horrible way I can think of because you stuck out your neck for me, and apparently there's nothing useful I can do to make up for that, so yes, that makes me a little upset."

"I didn't think…"

He hesitated as if searching for the right words. The silence stretched before he found them. "You told me a while back that no matter how awful I was to you, you'd still care if I got hurt. I figured that was joymancer-style bullshit. But you really meant it, didn't you? Even back then, when I was doing everything I could think of to make you miserable." A note of anguish had crept into his voice, more than he'd shown when talking about his broken body.

"Malcolm…" I didn't know how to answer that emotion.

He let out a ragged laugh. "I probably should have been the one getting down on my knees begging forgiveness, huh? I was the one too full of my own bullshit to see anything. I'd do it right now if I could get up."

I wasn't here to watch him beat himself up even more than his father already had. I groped for something to do, something to say, and could only come up with one thing that I thought might convey how much the sacrifice he'd made meant to me.

With as much care as before, I lowered myself farther down on the bed so I could bring my lips to his.

I hardly dared to do more than graze my fingers

against his jaw. The last thing I wanted was to cause him even more pain. But Malcolm kissed me back without any indication of being anything but pleased to do so, a soft but eager hum emanating from his throat.

It was the first time we'd kissed that wasn't part of some sort of competition or to make a point. A flutter tickled through the guilt and horror that was wound around my chest. When we had to come up for air, I stayed there on my side next to him, our faces just inches apart, watching his expression.

"Will he know if I cast magic on you that'll fade?" I asked.

"Probably not, and I doubt he'd check. I can't concentrate well enough to cast anything much. Why?"

"I can at least…" I inhaled slowly, thinking back to the few Physicality seminars when we'd covered basic medical spells. I could offer the magical equivalent of a mild painkiller. It'd only reduce whatever pain he was experiencing a little, but that was something.

"Dull," I murmured. "Numb." With the words, I sent some of the magic inside me over his body.

I hadn't realized just how stiffly he'd been holding himself until his stance relaxed, if only slightly. A pang that was a mix of relief along with frustration that I couldn't do more shot through me. I peered at Malcolm's face again as if I might find another idea there. He gazed back at me, as divinely handsome as ever. For a moment, it was hard to imagine I'd once thought of him as devilish too.

"You know," he said quietly, "it seems like an awful

shame that the first time I get you in my bed, I'm too fucked up to do much of anything about it."

Well, there was typical Malcolm. The devil hadn't disappeared completely. I let out a huff of breath without much real rancor. "If you weren't 'fucked up,' I wouldn't be in your bed."

"I know. Thank you—for coming, for wanting to help. For that spell just now. Even if you can't enchant me all better, it makes a difference." His dark brown eyes searched mine, turning serious again. "I'm not sure I really deserve you, Rory, but I don't think I could give you up even if I don't."

A lump rose in my throat. "Why don't you let me worry about that part?" I gave him one last brief peck to his lips, and then eased myself back into a sitting position. "And you'd better believe your dad won't be getting away with this."

A flicker of deeper concern crossed his expression. "Hey," he said. "We're going to deal with him—we're going to deal with all of them—when we're ready to really make the upheaval stick. Promise me you're not going to try to take him on right away. I stuck my neck out because I wanted to make sure you keep your freedom. Doing that won't mean much if you get yourself charged with attacking a baron, for real, less than a week later."

He looked so worried about *me* that the burn behind my eyes came back. As much as I'd have liked to turn Baron Nightwood's punishment or something equally torturous back on the man, I knew I didn't have the skills yet to go up against an experienced mage that powerful.

And forget about me—I wasn't going to do anything that'd make him come down even harder on his son.

"I promise," I said. "For now."

In the future, once I had all the power *I* needed and we had a plan we knew would work? All bets would be off.

CHAPTER SIX

Rory

L illian had kept her text short and to-the-point. *Casting Grounds on campus. 10:30am. Please be prompt.*

She'd given me some warning that she and her blacksuit colleagues would be coming by this morning, but the exact time just an hour in advance, while I was in the middle of an early seminar. I only had a little time to hustle back to my dorm after class to drop off the library book I'd been referencing for an oral report and grab a cardigan to guard against the drop in temperature I hadn't been prepared for. Then I paused to text Declan to give him a heads up about the meeting.

He'd keep an eye out for the blacksuits' comings and goings, and find an excuse to interrupt if I didn't contact him again reasonably soon to let him know the ceremony had gone as planned. As near-baron, he'd have the most authority out of the scions to intervene if Lillian had something else up her sleeve after all. I just hoped it didn't come to that.

When I ducked out of my bedroom, my friend Shelby was just emerging from hers into the common room with a swish of her mouse-brown ponytail. She beamed at the sight of me, keeping her hand on her door.

"Hey! Do you have a few minutes? I've been wanting to ask you—my professor asked me to work on a solo composition for part of our next performance, and I'd love to hear what you think of it."

I'd have loved to hear it, if I hadn't had Lillian's orders hanging over me. Shelby was a whiz on the cello, a talent that had gotten her access to one of Blood U's small non-magical programs. The school admitted a select number of Naries every year to give the fearmancer students practice at being circumspect in their powers—and targets for easily provoking fear to fuel those powers.

Shelby's lack of magic made most of my classmates look down on her, but it didn't make any difference to me when it came to our friendship. Unfortunately, it *did* mean I had to keep certain parts of my life secret— anything to do with my magic. And today's mission was meant to be secret from everyone.

"Sorry," I said, with a jab of guilt at the lie I was about to tell. I didn't think Shelby had ever lied to me, but I'd needed to so many times. "I've got to run to keep a meeting with a professor. But I can't wait to hear it. Maybe later this afternoon?" I hoped I'd be finished with Lillian's ceremony by then.

Shelby didn't look offended by my rejection, which only made me feel guiltier. "That works! A little more time to work on a few improvements."

A faint snort carried from across the common room. My head jerked around to see three of my least favorite people on campus, who I sadly had to share a dorm with, lounging on one of the sofas.

At my narrow look, Victory, who'd probably been the source of the sound, tossed her light auburn hair and looked away. Her attempts at harassing me had gotten increasingly intense over my first two terms at the university, but at the end of the summer, when her cat familiar had nearly devoured Deborah on Victory's orders, Malcolm had told her off and made it clear that if she hassled me again, she'd be up against him too. Since then, she'd stuck to sneers and a generally haughty vibe.

Her two accomplices, Cressida and Sinclair, weren't inclined to act without their ringleader. Sinclair made a show of rolling her eyes before turning back to her magazine. Cressida held my gaze for a few seconds before looking away, her expression more thoughtful than her friends'.

I couldn't say Cressida and I were becoming friendly, but she had gone on the record as a witness at my hearing. Her testimony that she'd heard Imogen's murder from the room below and then bumped into me on my way up to the dorm room afterward had been the only concrete evidence absolving me of the crime. To convince her to risk my enemies' anger by speaking up, I'd had to cast a spell promising her an undetermined future favor. I wasn't exactly looking forward to seeing how she'd call that in. From the looks of it, she was still thinking it over.

I tugged my attention away from that bunch and shot Shelby another smile before I headed out. As soon as I'd left Ashgrave Hall, apprehension started to well up inside me.

I was going to look for my birth mother today. Try to determine whether she was even still alive. And I had no idea what that would involve.

Lillian and her blacksuit colleagues were obviously still set on maintaining secrecy around my mother's possible re-appearance. The Casting Grounds was a large clearing in the western forest that the mage students used occasionally for large-scale spells, well out of the way of regular school activity. As I hurried across campus, I didn't see a single blacksuit. It was only when I stepped through the thinner ring of trees around the edge of the clearing that I found myself met by several of them, Lillian in their midst.

"Right on time," she said with a smile that looked a little tense. Was she worried that the ceremony we did today would prove my mother wasn't alive after all? Or that it would and she'd have to face the fact that she'd failed to realize her best friend had been imprisoned all these years?

"We're doing the spell here?" I asked, glancing around. "You'll have to walk me through it." Like the Shifting Grounds where Connar had shown me his dragon form, I assumed there were some kind of magical wards around the area to make sure the Nary students didn't stumble on it while in use. Presumably the blacksuits would activate them in a way that would repel everyone who ventured out this way. Beyond that, I couldn't even guess what Lillian would need.

Her assistant, Maggie, bounded from behind the cluster of blacksuits with her usual cheerful energy. She held up a cloth and a little jar of clear liquid in front of her petite frame. "We just need to wipe you down—not everywhere, but wherever you've got bare skin should do it —with this lavender-water mixture. It helps clarify the resonances."

When it came to whatever sort of advanced spell-casting they were conducting, I guessed I'd just have to take their word for it. Lavender water didn't *sound* dangerous. And when Maggie stopped in front of me and poured a little on the cloth, it did mainly smell like lavender.

If this was actually part of the barons' conspiracy against me, it was an awfully convoluted scheme.

I held myself still but wary, watching for any sign of malicious intent, as Maggie dabbed the damp cloth over my face, neck, hands, and calves beneath the hem of my dress. My skin cooled with the dampness, and I held back a shiver. Lillian followed the proceedings with an impatient vibe.

"You'll be more the conduit for the spell rather than an active participant," she told me. "By channeling your essence, we can reach out to the presence I've identified before and see if it resonates the way we'd expect for an immediate blood relative."

"So, I just... stand here, and the magic goes through me?" I didn't really like the idea of sitting back passively, especially when the people casting the spell included a woman who'd murdered a friend of mine and set me up for that murder.

My gaze slid to the blacksuits around her. How many of them had helped build the case against me? How many of them had wanted to see me convicted and my magic restricted in punishment?

"Essentially," Lillian said, brushing her hands together. "But you'll be conscious of everything we are. If it is your mother, you may sense her before the rest of us do, and you can add your own magic to ours to help direct it. I encourage you to do that if you feel a connection."

Okay. I had no idea what a connection to my birth mother would feel like. I wasn't entirely sure I'd recognize her even if she was standing right in front of me in the flesh, considering the most recent photos I'd seen of her were from seventeen years ago. She'd be in her mid-forties now instead of her late twenties. But we'd have to see how it went.

A pang of longing quavered through me to have the other scions here—any of them, all of them, any combination would have been fine. Just someone I knew would be looking out for me. But Lillian wouldn't have allowed that. Lord knew how she'd react if she found out I'd even told three of them this secret.

Whether my mother was alive or not, I was the heir of Bloodstone, the most powerful fearmancer family around.

I had to be able to stand on my own and deal with whatever my enemies threw at me.

Maggie finished applying the lavender water and drew back with a flash of a smile that looked uncharacteristically tight. Before I could give that much thought, Lillian was taking my arm and guiding me into the center of the clearing.

The last—and only—time I'd come out to the Casting Grounds, it'd been for a display of illusions. Malcolm and I had been locked in our game of provoking each other. Remembering that brought up a conflicted twinge.

Malcolm still wasn't back at school. He'd said it'd take a day or two before his father would heal him, and it'd only been one. But after seeing the lengths Baron Nightwood was willing to go to in order to discipline his son, I wasn't going to feel okay until the Nightwood scion had returned to campus with all his bones in one piece.

But I couldn't dwell on that now, not when I needed to see this ceremony through and stay on my guard.

"We'll arrange ourselves somewhat like your initial university evaluation," Lillian was saying. "The only difference is that there'll be six of us around you directing magic your way rather than four."

I glanced around, noting the other five blacksuits already stepping into position at equal distances around the edge of the clearing, leaving one spot for Lillian. I'd have expected Maggie to stay to watch, but I caught a glimpse of her chocolate-brown hair disappearing between the trees. Lillian must have sent her on some other errand now that she'd done her work here. I guessed she couldn't be that powerful a mage if she was working under Lillian rather than becoming a full blacksuit herself.

Lillian gave my arm a gentle squeeze. "It shouldn't take very long, but channeling the magic as it reaches across all that distance will tire you out. If we can't sense her after several minutes, we'll stop and try again another day."

I wanted to jerk away from her touch, but at the same time her words sounded genuinely concerned. Did she care what happened to me now that she might have to answer to my mom?

"Okay," I said. "I'm ready."

I closed my eyes instinctively, the way I'd been told to during the evaluation of my magic. Murmurs of castings reached my ears from around the clearing. The air shivered against my skin, and an almost electric tremor of energy pierced through my chest. My lungs clenched in resistance.

"Try to relax," Lillian said calmly. Her voice sounded farther away than I knew she was.

Try to relax, while she and five blacksuits were pouring magic into me? Easier said than done. But we did have to get this over with. I needed to know whether my birth mother was really still out there just as much as any of them did—probably even more.

I took slow, deep breaths, and the pressure in my chest eased. The electric jitter spread up through my body, nipping at my jaw, sizzling into my brain. Then it seemed to burst out the top of my head with a crackle through my scalp so tangible I was surprised my hair didn't stand on end.

My awareness stayed with that beam as it flowed out of me. The mages around me were urging it onward, off to the southwest, to joymancer territory. If those mages were holding my mother, she'd have to be in that general area. They wouldn't have been able to keep her presence a secret that long without having her surrounded by their power.

Flickers of other energy pinged off the stream of magic. None of them made enough impact for me to pay much attention to them before they were gone. The blacksuits didn't appear to think they were worth any notice. More magic flowed into my body, making my muscles tremble.

Yeah, I didn't think I'd be up for any marathons after they were finished with me today.

I got only vague impressions of the landscape we were crossing—a warming of the temperature, a dimming of sunlight as we left behind mid-morning for near-dawn. The hum of cities, vacant stretches of forest and farmland.

The forward momentum halted abruptly, wrenching my mind into place. I was still partly aware of my physical self in the Casting Grounds, my feet on the ground, the cool moisture on my skin. The rest of me felt the magic coursing through me, spreading as if in a vast cloud over the area where Lillian must have detected this uncertain presence before. It stretched and seeped through the air, twisting this way and that.

The fatigue that had started to affect my muscles tightened into a dull ache. Lillian had said the presence had caught her attention at specific times. I hoped she'd scheduled this ceremony well. I'd rather not feel as if I'd already run *ten* marathons by the end of it.

Somewhere on the fringes of my awareness, a sensation wriggled to me through the sprawl of magic. A tiny tug that reached down to the center of my magic... the same place where I felt my connection to Deborah, where it chafed at me when my familiar was kept apart from me for too long.

A connection. Lillian had said to watch for that.

Ignoring the ache taking over more and more of my body, I drew from my own store of magic and focused on that distant impression. What was it? *Who* was it? Could I really tell if it was—

My awareness brushed up against the sensation more closely with a waft of my own energy, and a jolt rang right through the middle of my chest. Cluttered images flooded my head, too vague to catch hold of, just flitting scraps of warmth and the lilt of a voice and a churning fury.

My eyes popped open before I could stop them. I staggered and found my legs wouldn't hold me at all.

As my knees gave, one of the blacksuits let out a shout. Footsteps thumped over. Lillian knelt beside me, catching me just before I sprawled flat on my back.

I stared past her toward the pale blue of the sky for several seconds, gasping for breath. Not just the memory of the impression I'd picked up on but the impression itself was still clanging through my senses as if I were still caught up in that rush of magic.

When I'd gotten ahold of myself, I eased upright with Lillian's help. She studied my face, hers taut with concern.

"I'm sorry," she said. "If we pushed you too hard…"

"No," I said with a shake of my head, which sent a wave of dizziness through me that might have proved that denial a lie. But even if the spell had left me out of sorts, I didn't regret it. It'd also left me certain.

So certain it made me nervous. What if those lingering sensations and the one that'd set them off weren't even real? As surreptitiously as I could, I brushed my fingers over my necklace, pressing the two points that worked together to activate the illusion-detecting spell.

No tingle of warning touched me. The charm simply gave off a faint warmth that let me know a little of the magic Professor Burnbuck had imbued it with had activated. But it hadn't brushed up against anything in or around me that was false.

Which meant… the things I'd felt were real.

"Rory?" Lillian said.

I wanted to see how she'd handle the situation before I gave anything away. I gazed back at her leonine face. Would I even realize if she was deceiving me?

"Did you find what you were trying to?" I asked. "Did you reach the presence you were looking for?"

She appeared to be analyzing my reactions just as closely. "We did. Just before you collapsed. You engaged your own magic, didn't you?"

She already knew the answer to that, obviously. I swallowed hard. "I felt something. I wanted to figure out what it was."

"And?" She paused. "Something about it seems to have resonated with you strongly."

I couldn't tell whether she had been able to sense the connection as clearly as I had and just wanted to see if I'd recognized it, or if she was honestly still uncertain. Maybe it didn't matter. I knew what I'd felt, down to my bones, and there was no way I could have denied it.

"Yes," I said. "My mother's out there. She's alive."

And if I wasn't mistaken, she was also very, very pissed off.

CHAPTER SEVEN

Malcolm

I had no idea what story my father gave to explain my injuries to the fearmancer doctor he brought in. Knowing him, he'd never have admitted to being responsible himself. A baron's heirs should stay well enough in line not to need any severe punishment. And a baron shouldn't reveal his disciplinary strategies to anyone outside the family.

No doubt the doctor formed his own suspicions but was wise enough to keep quiet about them. Whatever he made of my injuries, he tutted to himself a few times and then began a spell that prickled through my body like creeping vines, winding around my bones and fusing any cracks back together. The few larger breaks stung with sudden bursts of pain, but those faded quickly with his final casting.

"Take it easy for the next few days," he said to me before he left. "And try to avoid getting into this much trouble again."

Hopefully I wouldn't be in another situation where I needed to—at least not until the other scions and I could really challenge the assholes who were running things.

The biggest asshole—a.k.a., Dad—came into my bedroom a few minutes after the doctor had vacated it. I was still lying in my bed, reveling in the simple pleasure of having been able to roll onto my back for the first time in three days. He came up beside the bed and stood there gazing down at me with one of his impenetrable expressions.

"I hope this experience has given you plenty of time to think about how you can conduct yourself more wisely in the future," he said.

It didn't seem particularly wise to tell him that what I'd been thinking about more than anything while I'd been sprawled here staving off the agony was how satisfying it'd be to see his head ripped from his body.

"I'm not likely to forget any time soon," I said, which was true.

"Any steps you would like to take regarding the Bloodstone scion, if not on direct orders from myself or your mother, you are to speak to me about before proceeding. Any unusual behavior you see from her or any remarks she makes regarding the baronies, you'll report back to one of us. All of which you should have been doing in the first place."

All of which I *had* been doing up until a couple months ago, not that he'd ever seemed all that satisfied with my efforts then. And now that I knew he only gave lip service to the principles of honor and loyalty he liked to spout, I didn't see why I should owe him more than I did to the people who'd actually demonstrated those qualities.

I kept my mouth shut about all that too. "Of course. It was a rash decision in the spur of the moment. I should have thought it through more carefully. Is there anything in particular I should be watching for or contributing to when it comes to the heir of Bloodstone?"

What new malicious schemes have you got up your sleeve when it comes to Rory?

If he had any current plans, he mustn't have seen fit to tell me, just as he hadn't given me any details about what he'd been involved in before. Because even while he was urging on plots to frame the sole surviving member of one of the ruling families for murder, he knew he couldn't justify that kind of duplicity no matter how he framed it.

We policed our own families our own way. Taking shots at and undermining adversaries was fair play, but within certain boundaries. Even my father couldn't have denied that what he'd tried to do to Rory was treason.

"Just keep your eyes open," he said, and turned on his heel. "There are developments in progress."

Developments like the possible "avenue" I'd overheard him discussing with that blacksuit he had in his pocket? The woman—Ravenguard, that was her name—had been cagey about what exactly she'd been investigating that might help him or how it related to Rory…

Shit. I should have mentioned it to the Bloodstone scion when she'd come here. It'd been hard to concentrate between the physical pains and my surprise that she'd come at all.

The surprise, at least, had been pleasant. As Dad stepped out of the room, shutting the door behind him, I rolled onto my side again. Since yesterday morning, I'd been able to intersperse my imagined revenge on my father with equally enjoyable if very different memories.

The way she'd lain down right next to me, kissed me so carefully and yet with enough emotion to set me on fire…

It was a sweet sort of anguish, thinking back and wishing I'd been in a state where I could really have pulled her to me, have touched her, have set her alight in turn.

We'd get there. Maybe she'd never be completely mine, but she was starting to see more than just the, well, jackass I'd presented myself as at the beginning of our acquaintance. She was willing to give me that chance to make up for the shit I'd put her through. And that fact right there proved exactly why she hadn't deserved most of that shit to begin with.

I let myself linger in the recollection for a moment longer, and then I pushed myself out of bed.

The doctor might have melded my bones solid again, but that healing effort didn't change the fact that I'd been lying around for three days, barely even eating. My legs wobbled when I put my weight on them. I straightened up slowly, gripping a bedpost, and made my way over to my desk with cautious steps.

My phone's battery was dead, of course. I plugged it in and sat down in the chair while I waited for it to catch the initial charge. After a few minutes, a flood of alerts popped up on the screen.

Most of the texts were from my fellow scions, friendly asides and then more concerned messages at my lack of response. A smile slipped across my face looking at them.

During the time when I'd still been intent on breaking Rory and the other three guys had started to take her side, the pentacle of scions had felt fractured, with me increasingly on the outs. They hadn't involved me in most of their discussions about her hearing or whatever attempts they'd made to prove her innocence in the last couple weeks. But we were still our own sort of family. Maybe we could be a solid one again once I got back.

I sent a group text to all of them, including Rory. *Sorry for the radio silence. Phone issues. I should be back on campus tomorrow. Scion meeting in the lounge that afternoon?*

They'd know that my lack of response had nothing to do with my phone, but I wouldn't put it past my parents to be monitoring my recorded communications. Anything we wanted to discuss covertly, we'd need to do in person.

Declan the Ever Responsible was naturally the first one to respond. *We'll be glad to see you back. Sunday afternoon works for me.*

He knew to be circumspect too. I wasn't sure how, but he'd somehow managed to ensure the staff wouldn't mention his visit here to my parents. Dad grumbled enough about the Ashgrave scion and soon-to-be-baron without adding nosiness to his list of transgressions.

I shouldn't give the guy such a hard time, even in my head. Declan's dogged attention to detail was more likely to help us win whatever battles we had to fight against the older barons than anything the rest of us could offer.

I wavered for a minute over Rory's number, debating sending a private message just to her. But what could I say that would be safe and that would mean anything? I'd told her to her face how much it mattered to me that she'd taken the risk of traveling out here just to check on me. Anything else I needed to say, I could do it tomorrow.

As the last remnants of my painful punishment faded, my stomach let out an insistent gurgling. Dad's punishment hadn't left me with much appetite while I was in the middle of it, but now that I was out the other side, I'd probably recover faster if I got some food into me.

It was the middle of the afternoon, so the staff wouldn't have an official meal set out. That was fine with me though, because it meant I'd have the dining room to myself. I didn't really feel like facing my parents' scrutiny while I dug into lunch, or whatever exact meal this was.

Walking into the kitchen on my still shaky legs, I exchanged a nod with the guy wiping down the counters. He looked a little terrified at my presence. Without interrupting him, I took it upon myself to peruse the fridge. I didn't need help to assemble a perfectly good sandwich.

I layered on plenty of cold cuts and a good slathering of mayonnaise onto a couple pieces of rye, and carried that and a tall glass of sparkling lemonade into the dining room. Reaching for a more adult beverage didn't seem like the best idea in my current state. I wasn't sure I wanted to test how my temporarily weakened body would react even to caffeine, let alone alcohol.

I'd plowed my way through half of the sandwich when a slim form passed the doorway. My little sister glanced into the room, saw me, and froze for a second with a widening of her eyes that made my stomach drop.

What had Agnes figured out about what had happened to me? At the very least, she must have known that Dad was furious, that he'd prevented me from returning to school, and that I hadn't been in a position to leave my room even at mealtimes.

My parents had always hassled her just as much as they did me. They didn't believe in focusing all their energy on the most obvious heir. But she had no idea what hypocrites they were or how far they'd compromised themselves for whatever the hell their goals were.

And every time I did go back to school, I left her here alone with them and the tutors they hired. She wasn't quite fourteen yet—it'd be more than a year before her magic would emerge and she'd be able to at least escape to school like I did.

I motioned her over. "Hey! How's it been going?" Casual, warm, as if nothing all that horrible had happened. Let her see that Dad hadn't shaken me in any way that mattered.

She came over to the table but didn't sit down, her pale hands resting on the mahogany surface. "Everything's okay," she said hesitantly, and I mentally kicked myself for how little attention I'd given her since *I'd* made my partial escape five years ago. When we'd both been stuck here all of the time, I'd looked out for her more, and she'd confided in me more. This summer, I'd started offering some gestures to repair that relationship, but I had lots of making up to do here too.

Agnes bit her lip and then ventured, "How are *you?*" The emphasis and the anxious intensity in her gaze made the question much more serious than off-hand small talk.

"All good," I said in the same easy tone as before. "Just had some things to work out with Dad. I'll be around for the rest of the day if you need me for anything. I'm sure they've got you working hard on your lessons and all that."

"Yeah. I don't know. Some of the stuff…" She tugged at a lock of her blond hair and then managed a quick smile. "You probably don't remember it anymore now that you've gotten to go to the *real* school."

I smiled back. "You're welcome to try me."

The moment of connection faded, and she ducked her head, still looking too tense to sit down. I reached across the table toward her, letting my hand rest there until she raised her eyes to meet mine again.

"Listen," I said in a low voice. "I'm fine. I'm going to stay fine. No matter what they do, *we* still get to choose who we are and who we're going to be. You hear me?"

A hint of sharper anxiety flashed through her expression, but there was a hunger there too. She held my gaze as if searching for more certainty there. She might not totally believe what I'd just said, but she wanted to.

"Okay," she said. She probably didn't dare to say more than that. But she gave me one more darting smile before she slipped off again, and that was enough to satisfy me —for now.

CHAPTER EIGHT

Rory

Evening had fallen deeply during our trip. By the time Jude's red Mercedes crossed the bridge into Manhattan, the city lights glowed brightly against the growing darkness.

"It's a pretty quick jaunt from here," he said, scanning the traffic ahead of us. "I know a good route."

His tone was breezy, but his hand gripped the wheel tightly. I respected his privacy too much to attempt any dips of insight inside his head, but even though bringing me here had been his idea, I suspected he was nervous about showing me his apartment. The first home he'd picked out for myself.

I couldn't imagine finding anything to complain about there, given how much more luxurious most other fearmancers' tastes were compared to mine. Jude probably would have turned up his nose at the comparatively tiny house where I'd spent most of my life in California—or he would have before he'd adjusted his attitudes about Nary life, at least.

Knowing more about the joymancers and how their values had differed from what I'd grown up hearing from my parents raised questions I hadn't considered before. Had Mom and Dad's living situation, conducting themselves like normal people with average jobs, also been something specific to them? Did the other joymancers share that attitude, or did they accumulate wealth and flaunt it as much as the fearmancers did, in their own way?

That didn't matter right now. Right now, I was a little giddy knowing that I was the first person Jude was sharing the new place with.

"No need to rush," I said. "I'm happy right here."

So was Jude's familiar. The ferret had scampered around in the back seat burning off its apparently boundless energy for the first half hour of the drive, but not that long ago it'd slunk between the front seats and snuggled up on my lap like a very long, skinny cat. I stroked the soft but coarse fur between its shoulders, and it turned its head against my leg with an expression that looked nothing but content.

Jude shot us an amused glance. "Mischief isn't always that friendly. She's got good taste."

I laughed and gave her back another rub. "As long as she steers clear of *my* familiar, we can be friends."

I'd tensed up a little when I'd first seen the ferret in Jude's arms. My first month at school, he, Malcolm, and Victory had arranged a prank where I'd believed Mischief was attacking Deborah. I couldn't really blame the ferret, though, since Jude had egged her on—and he'd only given her an illusion of the mouse in the first place. She had a hunter's nature. And she was awfully cuddly when she decided to be.

I just wasn't going to bring Deborah around for any attempted reconciliation of familiars.

"Have you told the other guys you got this apartment?" I asked. I hadn't heard Jude mention it in front of them.

He grimaced. "I think that might prompt too many questions. Obviously it'll come up eventually."

"You're still not sure how you're going to tell them about your family."

"I'm not sure I'm going to have to tell them at all. If I don't have to, if I can just hand off the barony to the new kid…"

As he trailed off, his expression showed how torn he was. I reached over to touch his arm. "They're your best friends. Do you really want to keep a secret that important from them for your whole life? Do you honestly think they're going to care that much? You'll still be *you*."

"That's easier for you to say when you didn't spend your whole life tying your identity to a barony," Jude said with a crooked smile. "The whole reason we *are* friends is because we've been shoved together as scions since we were kids. They wouldn't need to include me if I wasn't one."

"You don't think they'd want to anyway?"

From his hesitation in answering that, he wasn't so sure about that either. I exhaled roughly. "From what I've seen, they like *you*. You all hardly talk about politics when you're together, and you still get along."

"Well, there's also the judgy aspect. Even if they don't want to see me differently, knowing I'm not actually a Killbrook is going to downgrade me in their eyes. They won't be able to help it." He made a flippant gesture in the air. "Hell, I can't say it wouldn't affect *me* if I found out one of them couldn't claim half of what we'd thought they could. Some ideas are ingrained pretty deep."

"So's your friendship," I said, but I wasn't going to keep pushing. "Anyway, you have time to figure all that out. I just wondered."

The smile he shot me then was a happier one. "For now, it's just you and me."

Mischief perked up as if she could tell we were almost at our destination. Jude took a turn at an intersection that brought us into view of Central Park.

This was my first time seeing the iconic location outside of pictures and video. I gazed at the sprawl of trees so avidly I almost didn't catch the jerk of Jude's head as he slowed the car by a tall, pale gray building.

"Everything okay?" I asked, looking around.

He peered out his window for a few seconds longer, his lips moving with an inaudible casting. Then he frowned and drove on toward the underground parking garage, which opened with a tap of a console on his dashboard. "No big deal," he said.

His stance stayed wary after he'd parked the car and gotten out, though. I grabbed the overnight bag I'd packed out of the back, and Mischief leapt into Jude's arms. We walked straight to the elevator, but his eyes kept flicking back and forth with a vigilance that made me nervous.

By the time the elevator let us off on one of the upper floors, he appeared to have relaxed. In the hall, he set down Mischief so the ferret could race toward the apartment and then glanced back at me—and his expression stiffened for just an instant before I caught up with him and he turned the other way again.

Before I could ask what was bothering him this time, he took on a jovial voice I could tell was partly forced. "Prepare yourself. You're the sole attendee of the grand opening of Jude's Apartment the First."

He swept open the door and ushered me into a soothingly modern space. The floors were a light peach hardwood, the furniture all soft neutral tones, the open-concept living area stretching from the front hall all the way to huge windows with a spectacular view.

In short, it was the complete opposite of the usual baron properties with their mazes of rooms and dark antique furnishings. It didn't feel quite like Jude yet, but I could see why he'd like it. Stepping farther inside felt like taking a deep breath of fresh air.

"It's lovely," I said, coming to a stop by the linen sofa. "You know the one thing it's missing, though? You need to rearrange things a little so you can fit a piano in here."

Jude brightened at the remark. His piano-playing was another secret he'd kept from his friends, something I'd stumbled on by accident that had ended up bringing us closer together... in various ways.

He motioned to one corner by the window that was

already a little emptier than the rest of the space. "That's the plan. I'm just working on finding the right instrument." He swiveled toward the kitchen area. "Do you want anything to drink? And we can order in dinner or go out—there are some pretty nice places within walking distance."

Did he really think he was going to distract me that easily?

I sat down on the arm of the sofa. "First, why don't you tell me what you're worried about? You saw something outside the building and then in the hall that you didn't like."

Jude made a face at me, but then he sighed. "Hold on."

He moved through the apartment, making a show of nonchalance, but I could tell he was examining pretty much every surface. He ducked into the bedroom and the bathroom before coming back to the sofa, where he flopped down next to me.

"It looks like my security efforts have kept the actual apartment safe so far, at least," he said. "It seems my father has been keeping a close eye on me since I officially 'moved out'."

A shiver ran down my back. "What do you mean?" I hadn't seen anyone else in the hall.

"I noticed a guy hanging around at school with a deflecting illusion on him so most people wouldn't even realize he's there. He's followed me around campus a few times. There was a woman with the same kind of spell standing outside the building next door when we drove up. And in the hall, there's an illusion covering a camera that wasn't there before—it's pointing toward my apartment. I wouldn't even have clocked that one if I hadn't been on high alert already."

I winced. "That's awful. What does he think you're doing that he suddenly needs to be following you around?" I paused. "Does *he* know that you know about your real father?"

"He shouldn't." Jude's posture slumped. "He might suspect, given the moving out. He's obviously decided that whatever my reasons are, he can't trust me. I just wanted to get away from him. Apparently it was too much to ask just to be left alone."

The frustration in his tone made my gut twist. He wasn't saying it, but we both knew that his dad's interference could escalate further. If he really believed Jude had figured out his treasonous secret, if he had any suspicion that his supposed son might reveal what he'd done... He might arrange for Jude to disappear completely, one way or another.

And with my current limited authority, I couldn't really protect Jude from that any more than I could have shielded Malcolm from his father.

Or could I?

I sat right down on the sofa so I could take Jude's hand and twine my fingers with his. The possibility had crossed my mind a few times before, but it hadn't felt urgent enough to bring it up. Jude had seemed sure his illegitimacy wouldn't be a real issue until his half-sister was born. But if his father was going to these lengths already...

"Jude," I said, "we could prove to him that he doesn't have anything to worry about, right? If... if I marry you, then you're not a Killbrook anymore anyway. You wouldn't be a threat."

Jude blinked at me, his eyebrows rising. "I'm sorry, I don't think I heard that right," he said. "Did you just propose to me?"

"Um, I..." My face heated. I looked down at our joined hands. "I'm not saying I really want to jump into getting married—to anyone. I mean, we're only nineteen. We haven't known each other that long. I just—" I made myself meet his bemused gaze again. "It seems like such a simple solution. And I know I'd rather make sure you *stay alive* even if it makes things complicated than hold off because it seems fast and then..." My throat closed up at the thought of the guy in front of me meeting some horrible death.

Jude shifted forward so swiftly I didn't have time to take a breath before he was kissing me, and then I was utterly breathless. I curled my fingers into the front of his shirt with a whimper I couldn't contain as he kissed me harder. When he eased back, not far, my whole body was buzzing with the passion of his embrace.

"You have no idea how much it means to me that you'd make that offer," he said, his voice low and rough. "I don't think you should have to throw your lot in with me that far before you're totally sure you want that kind of commitment, but I don't know if I'd be able to say no... except we can't."

It was my turn to blink at him. "What do you mean?"

The corners of his lips turned up. "Fearmancer law, specifically to stop over-eager young mages from leaping before they look. We can't get married in any way the barons will recognize until we've both graduated from the college. For me, that's almost two more years."

"Oh," I said with a weird mix of relief and disappointment. "I guess that makes sense. It doesn't help you, though."

"It's okay." Jude ran his hand over my hair in a fond caress. "I can't officially separate myself from the family before the baby arrives without creating some kind of chaos about inheritance, but as soon as she's here, I'll let my 'father' know I'm stepping aside. I'll sign a formal declaration. That should be enough. As long as no one ever tests my legitimacy as a Killbrook, which they shouldn't have any need to if I'm not angling for the barony..." He shrugged.

I didn't think he was as confident in his strategy as he was trying to sound. The impulse welled up in me to tell him about my own sort-of encounter with my birth mother this morning and all the conflicted emotions that had risen up with that contact, but I hadn't mentioned the specifics to any of the scions for a reason. Until we knew where she was and what the blacksuits were going to do about it, the situation was hardly real. I wasn't quite ready to deal with all the complications of that development just yet.

All I wanted was an evening away from that chaos with one of the guys I could call my boyfriend, as if my life was simple just this once.

"Well, if you do think of any way I can make a difference, don't keep quiet about it," I said.

"I know." Jude's smile turned wry. "I'm trying to keep the mess of my existence from poisoning yours as much as I possibly can."

The comment brought an ache into my chest. Even when he was joking around, he couldn't hide the fact that he still felt somehow a bit less compared to me, as if he were bringing me down by not being a scion, by having parents who'd lie about it. How could I prove to him that *I* didn't see him that way at all?

Maybe I couldn't convince him all at once, but I could keep showing him in every way I had at my disposal, over and over, until the idea stuck. And with the rush of his kiss still racing through me, I could think of one way that particularly appealed to me right now.

I stood up, tugging Jude with me. As I guided him toward the floor-to-ceiling window that overlooked the park, I trailed my hand down the smooth fabric of his shirt over his chest.

"You're not a mess to me," I said. "All of us got stuck with crappy circumstances one way or another. Even with all that, even with a father who treated you like garbage, you've still managed to become a guy that I'm *proud* to stand beside."

I nudged him another step back so his back hit the glass. Jude cocked his head at me, his dark green eyes lit with curiosity if not total faith in my words.

We were high up enough that the people passing through the glow of the streetlamps below were little more than blobs of hair, face, and clothes. None of them were likely to make us out in any detail unless someone turned binoculars toward the window. But it'd still serve to get my point across.

I leaned in to kiss him, as hard as he'd kissed me earlier. His hand rose to grip my waist, shifting the silky fabric of my dress against my thighs with a faint but delicious friction. It was him I meant to focus on, though.

Lowering my head, I pressed my mouth to his jaw. "The whole world can see that we're together and how much I want you, and I'm totally fine with that. Even if I'm not standing beside you but kneeling in front of you."

"Rory," Jude said in a ragged voice, somewhere between encouragement and protest. I was already sinking down, teasing my lips along his neck as I did, running my hands down his lean frame until one of them slipped over the buckle of his belt. When I brushed my fingers over his groin, he was already hard. He let out a soft groan as I traced the bulge of his arousal.

I came to rest on my knees, undoing his belt at the same time. He sucked in a shaky breath as I freed his erection from his pants. His hand caught in my hair, fingers tangling with the strands. They tightened as I lowered my mouth to take in the head of his cock. "Christ," he muttered.

It turned out Jude didn't have all that strong exhibitionist tendencies. I sucked him deeper, swiveling my tongue over the tender skin, and even as he groaned he managed to work out a casting word that flicked the living room lights off. Cloaked in darkness, we'd barely be visible at all to anyone outside. But that was fine. Actually being seen hadn't really been the point.

His salty flavor with a hint of the sharp scent that always clung to him filled my mouth. I worked him over as thoroughly as I could in my limited experience at this act, letting the head of his cock bump the back of my mouth and pressing my lips tight to add to the sensation. His hips started to pump in time with the hitch of his breath. My fingers delved into his boxers again to caress his balls, and a choked sound escaped him.

"Fuck, you're amazing," he said in a rasp. "I can't—"

His cock twitched in my mouth, and then Jude was urging me off him and tugging me up to face him. He dragged me into a sloppy kiss that was so urgent I didn't mind.

As his lips left mine, he flipped us around, spinning me in front of him at the same time so that I was leaning against the glass. I found myself gazing out at the park. He jerked up my dress and cupped my already damp panties to provoke a shock of pleasure. I hummed encouragingly, pressing into his touch. The brush of his cock over my ass made me shiver in anticipation.

"Since you like being on display..." Jude's teasing smirk carried through his voice. "Why don't we imagine the whole world is watching me launch you into the stratosphere?"

I might have balked if I'd really thought anyone could tell what we were doing, but in the darkness, pretending only gave me a thrill. He yanked down my panties and pulled my hips back against him. His fingers dipped down from my clit to tease over me as he whispered the protection spell.

My pebbled nipples brushed the glass through my dress. His cock came to rest against my slit from behind, and I couldn't hold back a whine of need.

"Jude…"

"Right here, Ice Queen." He thrust into me smooth and fast, the position giving him the perfect angle to hit the most sensitive spot inside me on the first stroke. I cried out, my head tipping forward to rest against the cool surface of the window. "Although God knows you're nothing like ice. Maybe I should call you Fire Queen from now on."

"You said you liked me wild," I reminded him, with another gasp as he hit that spot again. Bliss bloomed swift and heady from my core through the rest of me.

"I like you every way," he murmured. "But you can bring out that wild side any time you like."

The rhythm of his thrusts made my body rock against the glass. My breasts grazed it over and over, tingling with the sensation. Jude grasped my thigh harder as he drove into me with a harsher groan, and I trembled with the start of my release.

The wave of pleasure hit me so hard I saw stars amid the electric lights below. My breath stuttered. I reached behind me to clasp at whatever part of him I could reach, and he bowed into me with the spurt of his own climax.

Let the whole world see if they wanted to. For now, at least, this man was mine, and I was his, and anyone who tried to take him away would have to get through me first.

CHAPTER NINE

Rory

Now that Victory and her friends had agreed to an unspoken truce, using the dorm's common room was a lot more pleasant. Rather than slipping back into my bedroom with my lunch, I stayed at the group dining table.

Two of my dormmates whom I hadn't really talked to had already been eating their gourmet meals at the other end of the table. They both gave me a bit of a wary look, with shivers of nervous energy that seeped into my chest. Maybe not everyone was completely convinced I hadn't murdered Imogen after all. Oh, well. I could ignore that.

I was happily polishing off my mac-and-cheese when Shelby emerged from her room. At the sight of her limp as she headed toward the kitchen, my stomach sank.

"Are you okay?" I asked her when she reached the table. "What happened?"

Her gaze flicked to the other girls before settling on me. She gave me a tight smile. "It's no big deal. My knee's just a little sore. I tripped and fell on it badly yesterday."

I guessed I might have heard about that earlier if I hadn't been at Jude's apartment since yesterday evening. We'd only gotten back to campus an hour ago. Her story brought back memories of the bullying I'd witnessed between the fearmancer students and the Naries in the last couple weeks. The mages had always seen the Naries as easy prey to draw fear from, but lately their tactics had become a lot more overt, skirting the line of revealing our magic.

I waited until she'd assembled a sandwich and sat down kitty-corner from me. The two other girls dropped their plates in the sink with a clatter, leaving them for the maintenance staff to wash, and ambled off. I tipped my head closer to Shelby.

"What really happened—you tripped, or some jerk pushed you?"

She'd relaxed a little with the other girls' departure. "I don't know," she said. "It felt like something tangled around my feet, but there was nothing there when I looked. A couple of the regular students were nearby and had a good laugh about it, but they weren't close enough to have knocked me over. It was… weird." She gave a little shudder with a frown.

The fearmancer bullies were definitely going overboard in their current campaign against the nonmagical students. I poked at my last few pieces of pasta, wishing there was something I could tell her to get them to back off beyond the strategies Jude and I had suggested not long ago, but to some extent, my hands were tied by the necessary secrecy. I'd also been able to protect her some by enchanting the violin necklace she was wearing to deflect direct castings, but a conjured invisible obstacle on a path wouldn't be diverted by that.

"If your leg gets worse, definitely go to the health center and get it checked out," I said. The mages on staff there might be able to get away with applying a little magical healing that would look too obviously odd coming from me.

My phone chimed with an alert. Malcolm was announcing his return to campus. A tendril of relief rose up through my chest, even though he'd already reported his recovery, in not so many words, yesterday. At this point, I wouldn't have put it past Baron Nightwood to change his mind and detain his son all over again.

Everyone good to meet in the lounge in, say, half an hour? he asked.

I'll be there, I wrote back. The other scions confirmed within the next few minutes.

I wasn't totally sure what Malcolm wanted to discuss, but we hadn't really talked about the older barons' campaign against me in front of him before. After everything he'd been through to protect me from his father, he'd earned enough trust for me to let him in on those conversations. And I should probably fill all the guys in on the confirmation that my birth mother was alive.

I was just thinking that when my phone rang. Lillian's name and number appeared on the screen. My pulse jumped as I picked it up. Had they found out more about my mother's situation already?

"Rory," the blacksuit said briskly, with a hint of urgency she couldn't disguise. "I'm sending someone around to pick you up—they should be at the front of the campus in ten minutes. Whatever you're doing, I need you to drop it and meet them there."

"What?" I said. "What's going on?" She'd given me plenty of warning for yesterday morning's ceremony.

"I've gotten the impression that this is a good window for reaching out to your mother's presence so we can determine her location, but I'm not sure how long that window will stay open. We don't know when we'll have a chance this good again. You'll be there?"

She said it like a question, but I didn't see how I could say no. The other scions would still be here when I got back.

"Okay. Of course. Do I need to bring anything, or—"

"Just yourself. That's all we need."

She didn't even say good-bye, just hung up with a click on the other end of the line. I stared at the phone for a second, my nerves prickling.

It made sense that she wanted to get my mother out of whatever horrible situation she was stuck in as soon as possible, but the intense rush made me uneasy.

I gulped down the rest of my mac-and-cheese and rinsed the plate before adding it to the others in the sink. "Gotta jet," I said to Shelby. "Be careful out there."

She didn't need me to spell out that I meant in terms

of the other students, not her balance. She gave me a softer smile and a nod.

It'd been chilly when I'd made the walk from the garage to the residences this morning, so I grabbed a jacket from my room before heading out to the parking lot in front of Killbrook Hall. The breeze tugged at the fabric as I pulled it tight around me. It was a damp day, the sky gray with clouds and moisture lingering in the air, threatening rain that hadn't fallen yet.

I made it to the front of the hall five minutes after Lillian's call, but the car she'd sent pulled up at the edge of the lot just seconds later. A guy in the black dress shirt and slacks that made up the standard blacksuit uniform waved me in.

After the way the blacksuits had treated me over Imogen's murder, my legs balked instinctively. I forced myself to get into the back of the car. This didn't seem like the right time to pick a fight.

"Is there any particular reason we're not doing this at the campus Casting Grounds again?" I asked the driver as he revved the engine.

"Ravenguard will explain everything you need to know once we're out there," he said brusquely.

We tore down the road and through town. I texted a quick message to the guys to explain my absence from the meeting, just saying that Lillian had called me away. After that, I sat tensed, watching the buildings and the landscape beyond whip by.

So far it seemed everything I'd been told was legit, at least. The guy pulled the car over beside a few other vehicles at the edge of a fallow field several minutes outside of town. The quiver of magic in the air as I stepped out suggested someone had cast a repelling spell to keep Naries away.

Lillian, Maggie, and several other blacksuits were moving around the field, laying down small objects I couldn't make out. Conducting pieces of some sort? As I walked closer, I caught sight of one on the ground that seemed to prove that theory—it was a stone curved with an opening to a hollow at one end. Items like that could contain and amplify spells beyond what any given mage could manage on their own.

I couldn't make any sense of the layout in which they were setting them, though. The grass had been marked with spots of blue dye here and there, and a couple of the blacksuits were consulting a paper diagram as they stalked from one point to another. It took a couple minutes before Lillian even looked up and noticed I'd arrived.

"Good," she said, her gaze already darting away from me to someplace else on the field. "We'll want you there." She pointed at a larger mark in the midst of all the conducting pieces. When I walked over, I found a large one already resting in the grass there. To help conduct all that magic through me? To amplify it? The effort had been pretty powerful with just six blacksuits focusing their natural abilities on me the last time.

Maggie meandered over as the others continued their setting up, carrying more of her lavender water. "Don't worry," she said in an amused tone as she started to dab it on my uncovered skin. "They know what they're doing."

Yeah, but *I* didn't. "What's all this for? It looks a lot more elaborate than yesterday's ceremony was."

"Focusing in on a location is a much more complicated process than just getting a general ID." She tipped her head toward some of the nearer stones. "Using representations to stand in for major urban centers and so on, we can hone in faster and more precisely."

They were creating a sort of map, then. Without any boundaries of state lines or bodies of water, I couldn't tell what area it was mirroring. "Have they already figured out approximately where my mother is?" How large a territory would we be searching?

"Previous indications have made Lillian sure we should be looking at California or the edges of the neighboring states." Maggie glanced at me. "She might have been very close to you the whole time the joymancers had you."

The thought made my heart squeeze. Would my mother have had any idea I was nearby, being raised by the enemies who'd imprisoned her?

"Do you know how good an idea we'll get of her exact location from this spell?" I asked.

"Lillian is hopeful we can narrow it down to a city, maybe even part of a city. We'll need to go down there to get any more specific than that. At least it's a lot easier with you here. They tried making use of your grandparents to find you while you were still missing, but that connection isn't as strong."

And back then when my Bloodstone grandfather was still alive, no one would have thought to search for a woman they'd believed was dead.

"All right, time to get started," Lillian announced, and Maggie stepped back automatically. The senior blacksuit gestured to me as the others spread out around the clearing. "This will feel very similar to yesterday, though more intense. If you get a sense of your mother's presence, train your own magic on her too. And hold strong. The longer we can focus on her, the closer we'll get."

"Okay," I said, even as my gut twisted. All *her* attention was focused on locating my mother, whatever the cost, clearly. I didn't feel any of yesterday's concern for how the casting would affect me.

Lillian drew back to join the ring of her colleagues. Maggie had drifted all the way to the cars. I had the urge to protest somehow, but I didn't know what I'd be arguing for. It'd only taken a few hours for me to get my strength back yesterday. Today I was better prepared. And I didn't want the blacksuits to see me as someone easily shaken. So I steeled myself and shut my eyes.

My heart was thumping so hard I barely heard the low voices forming their casting in the ring around me. The cool breeze ruffled my hair, bringing the smell of damp earth to my nose—and then the surge of magic crashed into me like a thunderclap.

I stiffened my legs to keep them from wobbling. Power crackled through me from my toes to my scalp. Like before, it burst out of me through the top of my head, pulling some of my awareness with it over the gloomy field and far away across the country to the warmer, drier zones the joymancers called home.

My nerves quaked with dozens of tiny jabs already

splitting into my consciousness. It wasn't just power that rushed through me, though. Whiffs of emotion flavored the magic that was coursing into my body. Hope and anticipation, yeah, but also acerbic ripples of hostility and sharp tongues of anger that lashed at my awareness alongside the general thrum.

The blacksuits knew for sure now that one of their rulers had been stolen from them, hidden from them for nearly twenty years. And they were just as furious as I'd sensed my mother was. The vicious edge to their rage made my muscles shiver for reasons that had nothing to do with the impact of their spell.

How long would it take them to train that violence on the joymancers when they narrowed down their search for my mother? Were they going to go charging off ready to burn down everything between them and her the second this ceremony was over?

How many mages like Deborah who didn't even know about their prisoner would be slaughtered in their charge to get to her? How many Nary bystanders would be injured or killed? They wouldn't care about the nonmagical civilians any more than my fellow students gave a damn about Shelby.

Panic washed over me, even sharper than the fury pelting my senses. At the same moment, a wisp of the presence I'd latched onto before touched the edge of my awareness. My mother.

Two instinctive reactions, toward and away, collided in my head. I wanted to help find her. I didn't want to help dozens of people to be massacred.

My thoughts spun with the whirlwind of magic, and the panic overwhelmed me. My mind jerked back, my jaw clenched tight, and my nerves rang out with resistance.

The magic hurtling through me snapped away in an instant. The loss of it left me gasping for air. I swayed and tumbled forward onto my hands and knees. This time Lillian wasn't close enough to help catch me.

"What happened?" she said tersely, striding over. "We seemed to hit some kind of block—did you notice anything?"

She couldn't tell that I'd done it—that I'd shut down their spell. I fumbled for the right words to answer her.

"I don't know," I managed. "It just... felt wrong." That wasn't entirely untrue.

She swore under her breath and peered down at me. I tried to push myself back onto my feet, but my arms trembled at the attempt, barely keeping me off the ground. The spell had taken a lot out of me even in the short time it'd been active.

"We can't try it again now," she muttered. "We'll just —damn it. We were so close. Take the day to rest, but be ready. Next time we'll have to punch through even harder."

CHAPTER TEN

Connar

Six months ago, none of us scions had even known Rory existed. But in that short time, she'd left her mark strongly enough that I felt it even when she wasn't around. The vibe in the scion lounge just didn't sit right with all of us there except for her.

Of course, Malcolm's stormy pacing in front of the entertainment system didn't help with that.

"What could the blacksuits want with her *now*?" he demanded. "We can't just sit around while they might be arresting her all over again or Lord knows what else."

It might have been funny hearing that sentiment from the guy who'd been determined to crush Rory's spirit just a short while ago if genuine frustration hadn't rung so clearly through my best friend's voice. If I hadn't known just how awful a price he'd paid in the last few days for his decision to help her, one he'd shown no regrets about.

To look at him, I wouldn't have had any idea his father had hurt him, let alone as badly as Rory had described. Remembering the account she'd given us made my muscles tense all over again with the urge to pay Baron Nightwood back in kind, but Malcolm hadn't let a word or gesture slip that hinted at the torture he'd endured. I couldn't even be surprised by that. He'd never let anything shake him much—other than Rory.

I glanced at Declan, who was sitting in one of the armchairs with a cup of coffee in his hands. He offered me a thin grimace. *We* knew what the blacksuits would have wanted from the heir of Bloodstone, but she obviously hadn't said anything to Malcolm about her mother's possible re-emergence yet. And it wasn't really our place to tell him for her, no matter how much distress the current situation had put him in.

Jude sprawled even more languidly into the corner of the sofa and raised his glass with a clinking of ice cubes. He'd gone straight to the liquor cabinet when he'd come in —although I couldn't really criticize him for a little afternoon indulgence when I hadn't seen him actually drunk in weeks, and that had only been a brief lapse I still didn't totally understand.

"I think you should have a *little* more faith in our community's law enforcement rather than acting as if they might have stuffed her in the trunk of a car with the intent of leaving her in a ditch somewhere," the Killbrook scion said. "If Rory thought she needed help, she'd have told us. She looks after herself pretty well, as you of all people should know by now."

That was definitely a dig about Malcolm's past campaign against her. I watched my friend's expression carefully, but Malcolm only looked as if he'd suppressed a wince. I guessed he couldn't really get angry about Jude pointing out something undeniable.

"I think we have good reason not to totally trust the blacksuits too, after the murder fiasco." The Nightwood scion glowered at the floor and then dropped into the other armchair. "So, what? We just wait for her to get back? There isn't much point in discussing her safety if she's not here to contribute—and I know the three of you aren't going to want to tell me anything I don't already know without her go-ahead."

"We weren't completely sure where you'd stand on the subject until recently," Declan said mildly.

"I get it. It's fine. I'd rather hear it from her too. But she's not here."

"We could throw on one of the games for a while and see if she turns up," Jude suggested with a motion toward the consoles by the TV, but even he didn't sound convinced that would be a great way to pass the time.

Malcolm expressed what he thought of that idea with a huff of breath.

I looked around at my fellow scions, a thought rising in my head that I wasn't totally sure how to put into words. I wasn't usually the talker of the bunch, after all. I hung back and listened to what the rest of them said, and then put their ideas into action. But I'd had some decent ideas that had gotten things done in the past.

"Maybe it's a good thing if we have a little time to talk,

just the four of us," I said cautiously, feeling out their reaction. "About… how we're going to handle ourselves when it comes to Rory."

Declan considered me with a thoughtful expression that might have been a bit tense as well. I didn't think Jude or Malcolm had any idea about his more intimate relationship with Rory, however far that went beyond the interlude the three of us had recently shared. "What do you mean, Connar?" he asked, even though I suspected he'd already figured out the gist.

I suddenly didn't know what to do with my hands. I folded them on my lap in a position I hoped didn't look as awkward as I felt. "Well, we all care about her. A lot. And she obviously cares about us too. And that could be a little… complicated to navigate, going forward."

Malcolm folded his arms over his chest. "If this is about staking some kind of claim on her, I think she's already made it crystal clear that she's not planning on committing to a favorite any time soon."

She had—to me and Jude. And maybe to Declan too. When would the subject have come up yet with Malcolm? Had he already made some kind of move on her in the middle of his peace-making?

The possibility didn't even surprise me. Of course he would have. This was the heir of Nightwood we were talking about. When he wanted something, he went for it —and even when Rory had been frustrating the hell out of him, *he'd* been trying to stake a claim on her.

"That's not what I'm trying to do," I said. "I just think we should talk about exactly what we're doing here. How far we're going to take this. What it'll look like to our families and the rest of the community if it becomes obvious all four of us are involved with her—and how we're going to handle that."

I realized I'd made a slip a few seconds after the words came out of my mouth. Declan tensed in his seat just slightly, at the same moment as Jude sat up straighter, peering at the Ashgrave scion with his head cocked. "All *four* of us, huh? I seem to have been out of the loop."

Declan gave him a slanted smile. "Until a few days ago, any 'involvement' I've had with her could have gotten me into deep shit as a teacher's aide. And it could still get me in shit with the other barons. So there hasn't been a lot of acting on it, and what there has been, we haven't exactly been broadcasting widely."

Jude dropped his head back against the cushions with a chuckle. "She did say something about other guys, plural, when I first started taking her out, but I thought she was just keeping her options open, not talking about the actual current situation. But of course you got in there while you were being her white knight."

His tone was only lightly snarky. I couldn't tell whether he was actually annoyed by the news or just hassling the other guy. Declan seemed to take it as the latter.

"We do have to handle our relationships with her carefully," he said, moving on to the core of the matter with his usual academic precision. "I think *some* closeness among the scions won't raise eyebrows, and the fact that she's been dating both you and Connar hasn't caused any real problems... but three guys at once, or four..." He considered Malcolm, apparently not sure of how deep the Nightwood scion's involvement ran either.

Malcolm shrugged. "Whatever happens between her and me, I have no problem keeping it behind closed doors. I've never been interested in making a big show out of my private life. Neither have you, as far as I can tell. So, there you go. Problem solved."

"It's not just that," I broke in. "It's—We all know this isn't going to last, right? Or do we? I know *I* can't ever offer her anything permanent, because I'm the only Stormhurst scion left. I can't leave the barony to be tossed into the hands of some mage at random." That was what happened if there were no blood heirs left. When the last baron of a family line stepped down, the heart of that family's power would arise in some other mage it deemed worthy by standards no one really understood.

"No one thinks you should," Declan said gently.

That wasn't the point. My stomach clenched. "I guess any of the rest of you could make the decision to step down. You all have younger siblings, or you're going to. *Are* we all on the same page? Because if one or more of you would seriously consider giving up your own barony to be with her... Maybe I should back off and get out of the way of whoever of you is willing to make that kind of commitment."

"Conn," Malcolm said, sounding startled. When I looked at him, his expression was almost pained. Then his eyes flashed with the ferocity he brought to bear any time he sensed someone in our pentacle was threatened. "You don't have to give up your happiness for anyone else. *She* shouldn't have to give up what she has with you if she doesn't want to. It's not like we're anywhere near the marriage stage anyway."

Even after everything I'd told Rory about how much Malcolm had done for me, how he'd always looked out for me, I'd honestly expected him to be happy at the thought of less competition for Rory's attention. His protectiveness turned the tightness in my stomach into a softer ache.

"I just figured it would make sense," I said. "For her to be spending more time seeing how well she connects with the people who can actually offer her something in the long run. If any of you thinks you would offer that."

I glanced around at my fellow scions. Declan's mouth had twisted. "I can't," he said. "I've been upfront with her about that from the start. I've put too much into getting where I am—and there's no way I can dump all the responsibility onto my brother's shoulders."

Jude had shifted into an oddly defensive stance, his knuckles paling where he gripped his glass. "I can't really make any evaluations based on a sibling who hasn't even arrived yet," he said with unexpected tartness. Was he offended I'd even suggest that he might give up his position? It was so hard to tell with the Killbrook scion and his erratic moods. Something about the conversation appeared to be bothering him, anyway.

Malcolm leaned back in his chair. "I've been preparing for the barony for a hell of a long time too. Rory's better off with us beside her in the pentacle than playing house at home. That doesn't mean we can't make the most of the time we have before we need to think about heirs of our own."

We were agreed, then. We wanted everything we could have with Rory right now... but we understood that eventually we'd have to give our more intimate relationships with her up and go back to just being colleagues. I should have been relieved that we were all on equal footing, that we'd talked through the situation, but for some reason my chest had constricted.

I didn't want to have to give her up. I wasn't sure I'd ever really wanted the barony. I sure as hell hadn't planned to fight for it. If my brother Holden had wanted it, if my parents could have let us just decide instead of forcing us into that horrible fight... I'd have given it to him in a blink.

But now I couldn't. Because of how badly *I'd* hurt him.

Malcolm was right, though, as he was about most things. We could do more to support Rory by taking our baronies and working together with her than leaving her to fend for herself with other uncertain heirs.

"Well," Jude said, setting down his glass on the coffee table with a solid thump. "We're settled then. Our futures mapped out, our present accounted for." He shot us all a smile that still looked tighter than usual. "I've got a godawful assignment to finish before tomorrow. Give me a holler when we're ready for a meeting with all the scions."

He sauntered out of the lounge without a backward glance, leaving me wondering if we were entirely united after all.

CHAPTER ELEVEN

Rory

What *happens next?* Deborah asked when I'd told her about the failed attempt to locate my birth mother.

"I guess I just wait for Lillian to call on me again." I tipped back my head in my desk chair, giving her back a little rub where she was perched on my knee. The view out the window looked ominous. The clouds had thickened and darkened, but no rain had fallen yet. Flecks of white gleamed on the lake—froth from the waves tossed by the rising wind.

What was I going to do when we went through the locating ceremony a second time? The memory of the anger I'd felt surging through me from the blacksuits left me queasy.

My mother was out there, and I wanted to get her out of whatever prison the joymancers had her locked in...

but I also didn't want to be responsible for unleashing that kind of fury on far more people than those who deserved it.

Whatever the Conclave did with your mother, you can be sure they felt they had good reason—

"It doesn't matter," I said, cutting her off. "The way they went about it was incredibly shady, and let's not forget they kidnapped me at the same time. And not because they wanted to give me some better life. *You* know the Conclave wanted to keep me more like a prisoner. I wouldn't have had a better life at all if my parents hadn't stood up for me."

And look at how the fearmancers repaid them for that kindness.

My jaw tensed. I still hated the brutality the blacksuits had inflicted on my adoptive parents. Mom and Dad *hadn't* deserved that. But... that didn't give the joymancers a free pass to do whatever they wanted to any fearmancer they got their hands on.

Before I could answer my familiar, a knock sounded on my bedroom door. I swiveled my chair to face it. "Yes?"

"It's Maggie Duskland," a familiar bright voice said, maybe a little more subdued than usual. "Lillian wanted me to follow up on your last... conversation."

They were still keeping my activities with the blacksuits secret, even though we were sure of my mother's continued existence now. Had they even told the barons yet?

Deborah scurried down my pantleg, and I got up to answer the door. Maggie beamed at me the second I opened it, but her gaze slid past me to eye the room beyond. How long had she been standing there before she'd knocked? I'd been keeping my voice low, but had she managed to hear me talking to Deborah anyway?

"Do you have a few minutes?" she asked, her attention coming back to me.

Her smile hadn't faltered, but I still didn't like the idea of welcoming her into the closest thing to a private space I had on campus. While she was only Lillian's assistant… that still meant she was an assistant to a woman who'd conspired against me and murdered an innocent student. Lillian wouldn't have picked her if she hadn't thought their morals aligned well enough—and that Maggie was sharp enough to take care of whatever Lillian needed taken care of.

"Sure," I said. The common room was hardly private, so I stepped right out and tilted my head toward the main door. "We could take a walk?" I doubted anyone much would be hanging around on the green or the fields in this gloomy weather.

Maggie's expression tightened for a second, but she turned without a protest. "That works."

She studied me as we headed down the stairs. "You seem to have recovered quickly."

An ache lingered in my joints, and I wouldn't have wanted to sprint anywhere anytime soon, but I could walk steadily enough, if that was what she meant. "The worst of the effect doesn't take too long to wear off, thankfully," I said. Had she expected me to still be wobbling on my feet hours later?

She hummed to herself and didn't say anything else. When we stepped out onto the green, the damp wind licked through her dark hair and tossed my own into my face. I shoved the strands behind my ears as well as I could, wishing I'd brought an elastic.

As I'd expected, the green was empty except for a few students hustling between the Tower and Killbrook Hall. Maggie veered past Ashgrave Hall toward the wider field beyond. I kept pace with her, waiting for her to get started on whatever she'd come here to talk about.

"Before the spell was cut off," she said, just loud enough for me to hear, "you said you hadn't sensed anything definite on the other end. Now that your thoughts have had more time to settle, have you remembered anything more than that?"

I couldn't be completely sure that the faint impression I'd gotten had been my mother. I definitely hadn't sensed any other presence. "No," I said. "Sorry."

"What about your awareness of the magic? Do you remember anything changing about it beforehand—in a way that didn't happen during the first ceremony?"

"No," I said again. The only thing that had changed was how willing *I'd* been to continue acting as a conduit. Why had Maggie come all the way out to campus to rehash the same things Lillian had asked me in the moment? If the blacksuits had just wanted to double-check, wouldn't she have simply called me?

The young woman looked at me then, with an intentness I hadn't seen from her before. "You must be pretty disappointed that our chance at locating your mother was foiled."

I wasn't going to get into my tangled emotions on that subject. "Lillian said we'd be able to try again soon," I said. "I'm trying not to dwell on it. I didn't even know she might still be *alive* until a few days ago."

Her tone turned casual. "But it'd be such a good thing, wouldn't it, if we could bring her back? You wouldn't have to be pushed right into the barony—you'd have someone in the family to guide you."

That wasn't what I'd have thought the main benefit would be, especially considering my mother had no idea what had been going on in the barony over the last nearly two decades. Having someone who might stand up for me to the other barons was more my priority—if I could count on Baron Bloodstone for that.

I eyed Maggie but couldn't read any definite intent, friendly or malicious. "Yeah," I said, because I might as well be agreeable about it. "Mostly I just don't want her stuck in some prison dealing with whatever else they've been doing to her for any longer."

"Well, who knows how they've been treating her. You seem to have come out all right."

I shot her a sharper glance then, my spine prickling, but she kept up the same soft smile. "I hadn't done anything they could blame me for yet," I said. "They could lie to me about who I was so I wouldn't know there was any reason to fight about it. It can't have been anywhere near as easy for her."

I couldn't tell whether the answer satisfied Maggie. She

nodded and pulled out her phone to check something. "At this point, we expect our best chance for making another try will be Tuesday morning. Lillian or I will be in touch to confirm beforehand."

That was all she'd come for, apparently. I watched her head back toward the parking lot, uneasiness still jittering through my nerves. None of the blacksuits had suggested the ceremony's failure was my fault. Did Maggie suspect after watching from the sidelines?

How deep shit would I be in if I threw off the next one and someone realized it for sure?

I didn't really *want* to keep throwing things off, did I? I'd just panicked in the moment. And now maybe the blacksuits would have a little more time to adjust to the knowledge and approach the problem logically rather than tackling it with vengeance at the forefront of their minds.

The wind lifted again, tickling goose bumps up my arms, but I felt too restless to go back to my dorm just yet. I ambled on across the field to the rippling lake.

The waves hissed against the dock's supports as I walked onto it, the weathered boards creaking softly under my feet. I sat down at the end where all I could see was water and trees, as if the campus behind me and the world it represented didn't even exist.

Today the world of water and trees was a little cold for my tastes, though. I sat there for a few minutes and then got up to head back to the buildings. When I turned, I froze at the sight of Malcolm just reaching the foot of the dock.

He stopped too, looking abruptly hesitant for just an

instant before his usual cool confidence smoothed over his expression. In the dim daylight, his hair looked more bronze than gold. He ran his hand over it as he waited for me to approach.

"I saw you on your way down here," he said when I reached him. "You missed the meeting—is everything okay?"

I spread my arms as if to present myself. "I made it back."

Standing in front of him, I didn't totally know how to act. The memory of the last time I'd seen him and the welcome contrast of him being able to stand at all sent a pang through me, but at the same time seeing him like this made it a lot easier to flash back to the many moments since I'd come to Blood U when he'd treated me like an enemy. That history hadn't disappeared no matter how many other sides to him I was aware of now. Still, I decided to add, "I'm glad you did too."

"I told you I'd be fine." His tone was nonchalant, but he smiled with a warmth that tugged up other kinds of memories—the crash of his lips, the press of his body against mine.

He glanced around. "There are a couple things I wanted to tell you—but maybe we should get out of the weather? We could…" He trailed off as his gaze settled on the boathouse.

My first instinct was to balk, but I pushed past it. If I was going to be friends or anything more with Malcolm, being in that space with him alone again would be the best possible test of how ready I was.

"That works," I said. "Just to *talk*."

His lips twitched at my emphasis. "You don't have to worry about that."

It was a very different atmosphere anyway, walking into the boathouse out of the gloom rather than a hot clear day, fully dressed rather than in a bikini—and without days of pent-up sexual desire roiling around inside me. With the walls sheltering us from the wind, it was warmer if not drier, and Malcolm's flick of the light switch cast the space with an amber glow.

I picked an overturned bucket to sit on, far from where we'd had our summer encounter. Malcolm grabbed a small stepladder off the wall and unfolded it to use as a stool. He set it a few feet away from me, leaving plenty of distance.

"I should have told you when you came to see me, but I wasn't really concentrating all that well right then." He made a face. "After you were arrested, I started poking around in my dad's business, trying to see what I could find out about how he might be involved. He's pretty careful, so I didn't get very far, but I did come across some evidence that he'd been following your schedule at school for one reason or another."

"That doesn't surprise me." But it wasn't all that incriminating either. I paused and then said, because I'd meant to acknowledge this during the scion meeting anyway, "I *know* he and the other older barons are behind the various attempts to hurt me, Malcolm. Not in any way I can prove, but my mentor died so he could warn me about them. If you find anything that I could bring to the blacksuits… or whoever the right authorities would be… I can use that, but I don't need any more convincing."

He paused for a moment as that information sank in, but he didn't look particularly surprised by it. "All right," he said. "Just so you know, I don't need more convincing either. And I'll keep watching for whatever I can make out of his plans. That was the other thing—he was talking to one of the blacksuits after your trial, a woman named Ravenguard— something about a new development she was pursuing but from the sounds of things hadn't totally filled him in on yet."

Ah. I could guess what that had been about. I bit my lip, wavering about whether I should tell him. But the other guys already knew, and how could we really work together as a pentacle of scions if we were still keeping one member partly in the dark? Malcolm was proving his loyalty to us—and to *me*—over his father all over again just by telling me this.

"She was probably talking about the same thing that got me called away earlier today," I said. "That's Lillian Ravenguard—she was apparently one of my mother's closest friends when they were younger. And… she's found evidence that my mother is still alive, in joymancer custody. They faked the murder and took her when they took me. I've been helping them with their spells as well as I can while they try to narrow down her location."

Malcolm's eyes widened. "Are you fucking kidding me? All this time, the joymancers made everyone think— they've kept her locked up somewhere— For fuck's sake. The bastards."

"Yeah," I said, but my hand instinctively rose to my dragon charm. My one piece of solid evidence that *some* joymancers had been willing to treat a fearmancer like a human being.

Malcolm's gaze snagged on my necklace. His eyes darkened.

"How can you still wear that?" he demanded. "After everything they did to you, after what they've done to your mother, after everything I told you about how they harass us—you still want to wear some joymancer memento as if you're more loyal to them than us?"

My fingers closed tighter around the charm, careful not to activate the illusion-detecting spell unnecessarily. My shoulders stiffened, but I managed to keep my voice steady if tight. "This isn't a memento of the joymancers. I've got no loyalty to them. It's a memento of my parents, the only ones I got to know—the ones who *protected* me from how at least some of the other joymancers wanted to treat me. If that isn't love, then I don't know what is. When I got here, that bracelet was the only thing I had left that they gave me. And now this charm is the only piece of that I still have. So yes, unless you manage to force me into breaking this too, I'm fucking well going to keep wearing it."

Despite my best efforts, my voice broke over those last words. My eyes had gone hot. I gritted my teeth against the threatening tears.

Malcolm went rigid on his seat. His mouth twisted, and all at once he was shifting forward, his knees hitting the floorboards, his head bowing so the fringe of his hair brushed my own knees.

"That's two times in the last week now I've seen you close to crying," he said roughly. "At least the first time it was *for* me instead of *because* of me. Maybe I'll just keep bowing down and see if that stops me from getting my head up my ass. I didn't know—and I didn't know because I never bothered to ask—and that's been my problem the whole time, huh? So, here you go, I'm on my knees, like I said I should be."

The grief for my parents and the horror of remembering the time he'd magically persuaded me into smashing the charm bracelet formed a lump in my constricting throat. "I didn't ask you to," I said.

He looked up at me, still on the floor before me, his gaze so fathomless I couldn't tear my eyes away. "Maybe you should. Maybe you should start asking for a whole lot more than you have."

I swallowed hard. "It's done now. It happened, and it was awful... but it's over. I'm not going to hold it over your head forever. *You* brought it up."

His chuckle came out raw. "Fair. I just— Fuck, Rory, everything in me is screaming to destroy the asshole who put you through the agony I could see on your face... but the asshole is me."

"I don't know," I said. "I think you've been doing a pretty good job of destroying that asshole since you got started on it, even if it's been kind of a slow process."

"Rory..." His hand slid up my leg, and mine reached down to grasp his fingers. At my tug, he eased up over me, leaning close. The heat of his body flooded me even though there were still inches between us. And there was that familiar clang of desire, more than I was totally sure I wanted to let out.

He brushed his fingers over my cheek. "Tell me I can kiss you."

It was a question more than a command. A direct counterpoint to the way he'd barged in and simply claimed my mouth that time before. My throat unlocked.

"Kiss me," I said quietly.

He crossed that last gap to bring his lips to mine. A thrill shot through me even though this was nothing like the kisses we'd exchanged here before. Or maybe because of that. He was pouring himself into the moment in a way he hadn't been able to in his broken state when I'd come to his bedroom, but with a careful tenderness that told me he'd have jerked back the second he caught any sign of anxiety from me.

Earning back the trust he'd shattered, one step at a time.

I traced the line of his jaw as I kissed him back, and a pleased sound emanated from his chest, but he pulled away a few seconds later. "*I'm* not going to ask for more just yet," he said. "Let's leave this moment on a high note."

I couldn't argue with that. But as I got up to follow him out of the boathouse, my chest twanged with the realization that my feelings for the Nightwood scion had somehow gotten even more tangled than they'd been before.

CHAPTER TWELVE

Rory

The expected message from Lillian came around eight o'clock Monday night, just as Declan and I were leaving the restaurant where he'd taken me to dinner. I peered at my phone in the yellow glow of the streetlamps.

Second attempt tomorrow morning. Be ready for pick-up at 10am.

My heart sank and skipped a beat at the same time. I was going to have to face the exact same dilemma I had yesterday—but it might end with concrete information about where my birth mother was now.

"Everything okay?" Declan asked, watching me.

"We're doing another ceremony to try to locate my mother tomorrow," I said, tucking the phone back into my purse. Earlier today, I'd filled him and the other scions in on the progress Lillian had made so far.

He studied my expression. "And you're still uneasy about that."

I made a vague gesture as we walked down the street to where he'd parked his car. The sweetness of the chocolate cake I'd had for dessert was starting to turn bitter in my mouth. "I just have no idea what's going to happen once we find her… but I'm pretty sure it's going to be brutal. And I'm the deciding factor in whether they get that information."

"Do you want to walk together and talk it through?" Declan asked.

"That's not exactly the most romantic way to spend a date."

The corner of his mouth quirked upward. "Well, maybe after you've gotten it off your chest, you'll find it easier to focus on the romantic side again."

He might have had a point there. My gaze slid over the other figures ambling along the street in couples and small clusters, and my skin tightened. We'd driven out to a town about an hour away from campus so we could have this date—our first real date—with much less chance of our classmates running into us. But the thought of discussing a subject this fraught with so many people around, even Naries, made me itchy.

"Not here," I said. "If we could get out of town…"

"There's a place with some hiking trails between here and campus. I doubt anyone will be making much use of them at this time of night."

"That sounds perfect." Off in the middle of nowhere,

with no need to worry about anyone overhearing or anyone even noticing us.

The spot was only a ten-minute drive outside the town. Declan pulled off onto a gravel drive that led to a small, empty parking lot dotted with weeds. Obviously these paths didn't get a whole lot of use even during the day.

The leaves on the scattered trees rustled as we got out. The air was still damp, only a thin sheen of moonlight penetrating the clouds that hadn't let up since yesterday. Declan retrieved a flashlight from his glove compartment that he turned into a little lantern with a couple of clicks. He nodded to the dirt path that veered away from the parking lot between the trees.

We walked for the first few minutes without speaking, no sound except the leaves and the rasp of our shoes over the ground. Now and then a creature scurried off into the brush with a faint tingle of fear that I absorbed.

It was strange thinking that I used to get most of my magical fuel from walks like this, dribs and drabs wafting from the local wildlife. Now enough power churned behind my sternum that I never worried I'd deplete it, mainly thanks to the fears my mere presence had started to spark in my classmates.

If they were that scared of me simply based on my family name, how afraid should I be of my mother, knowing what most of the other barons were like?

When my nerves had totally settled with the sense of being alone and away from observation, I dragged in a breath. "The blacksuits are going to go break my mother out. There's no way they won't. There's really no other option. But I don't see how that can happen without tons of people getting hurt along the way. I can't imagine them even trying to negotiate first." Not that I had much faith the joymancers would have gone along with a negotiation anyway.

"I can't fault them for that," Declan said. "If they tip the joymancers off that they've discovered what happened to your mother, they'll take steps to prevent a rescue— move her, increase security…"

"Yeah." I'd thought of that too. I groaned and rubbed my arms, generating a little more warmth beneath my thin jacket. "It's just such a messed up situation. I don't know if anything I can do will make a difference once they've got a location."

"She's your mother," Declan said. "They've wanted you to be involved this far. They shouldn't be able to just shut you out after that. I don't know how much impact you'll be able to have over their strategies, but at least you can be there and watch for chances to aim for a less violent outcome."

That was true. I held that possibility in my chest with a flicker of hope. Maybe not a large flicker, but better than nothing.

I hesitated for a moment and then allowed myself to admit, "It's not just the part about breaking her out. I don't know how to feel… about having her back here, back in my life, in general. I don't remember anything about her—and even if I did, that was so long ago and she must have been through so much. What's she going to expect from me? What's going to happen with the pentacle of barons once she's back and they can go ahead with their planning without needing my approval?"

"They'll have a lot less reason to attack you," Declan pointed out.

"Well, yeah—unless she isn't dancing to their tune either, and they use me to threaten her."

Declan shook his head. "She wouldn't let them get away with that. What they've already done to you in secret they're *keeping* secret because it's the worst kind of treason. If she had any idea the other barons were undermining her family to get their way—there'd be hell to pay."

He said that with so much certainty that I gave him a curious look. It hadn't really occurred to me before that I might have a trusted source on my mother's character, since I knew Lillian would only give a positive report, but while Declan wasn't likely to remember much more than I did about her, he'd been around the other barons for a long time.

"Have you heard much about her?" I asked. "Have the other barons mentioned her: what policies she supported, how they felt about her, how well they got along—or didn't?"

The light shifted over Declan's face with the swing of the lantern in his hand. He took his time considering the question.

"It's hard to say, because anything I've heard is based on who she was ages ago," he said. "Even if she *hadn't* been imprisoned all that time, she might have changed her perspective over the years. She'd only been baron for a little while. She and my mother were the last ones to join the new pentacle as their parents stepped down—other than Connar's mother with that upset of power."

"I know, but it'd still be useful to get some idea what she was like."

He rubbed his mouth. "I know she and Malcolm's dad were pretty close. The other barons have occasionally lamented her absence and how much easier things would be if she were still around. And my dad's mentioned a few times over the years that my mother felt like there wasn't much room for debate, because the two most powerful families could bulldoze over any objection together. I don't think *she* was ever very friendly with your mother. But I don't know exactly what they disagreed on."

That lined up with the university photos I'd seen in the album I'd found on the Bloodstone country property nearby. My mother had looked awfully happy to be hanging out with the future Baron Nightwood—and the few pictures Declan's mom had made it into, she'd been off to the side, noticeably tense.

But that was in matters of politics, of course. I had no idea what my mother would have thought of anyone's child-rearing practices. And I didn't really know much about Baron Nightwood's politics other than he wasn't above breaking the law when it suited him… and he shared the usual fearmancer disdain for Naries.

I kicked at a stray rock. "Have you been able to get a better idea what changes exactly they want to push through so much?"

"No. I don't even know if they're still after the same

goals they were back then. They must have *some* different priorities after all this time."

I glanced at him, catching a bit of exasperation in his tone. "Do you think they're going to accept you as a baron even after you've graduated and it's all official? They can't keep shutting you out of their discussions forever, can they?"

"I guess we'll see." His lips set in a grim smile. "I'm not sure they didn't treat my mother the same way. The Ashgraves have been black sheep among the top families for at least a few generations simply because we don't bother to play the status games quite as much and we take a more friendly attitude toward the Naries. But they can't cut us out completely, not when we're magically bound to the pentacle."

"It'll get better," I said. "When the rest of us scions can start taking our spots, we can really start changing things. I don't think even Malcolm wants to rule like that."

"Neither do I," Declan agreed. "I just..." He trailed off, shutting his mouth with a clenching of his jaw.

"You just?" I prodded.

"I feel kind of traitorous even admitting it. But this isn't the career I'd have chosen if I'd gotten to choose. I'm glad I'm part of the pentacle to be some kind of moderating influence, and maybe I'll make a difference in the long run, but so far... It's decided every aspect of my life, you know? Every action I've taken since I was a kid, I've had to consider how it'll fit into claiming my position, keeping the authority I need to maintain. I think a guy like Malcolm gets something out of the sense of power that comes with the role, but I don't exactly enjoy being domineering."

I elbowed him lightly, remembering the confidence he'd exuded when he'd gotten me out of the blacksuits' custody. "And yet you look so good when you're ordering people around."

A hint of a proper smile came back. "Practice makes perfect? I shouldn't complain. There are thousands of fearmancers who'd give their right hand to trade places with me and become baron. Sometimes I get tired of the constant political maneuvering, is all—and it's several years still until the current barons start retiring."

"That's understandable. I'm tired of the power plays, and I only got here five months ago." I reached to grasp his free hand. "I wish my arrival had taken some of the pressure off you instead of multiplying the things you have to worry about."

"Hey." He squeezed my hand, looking down at me with affection so bright in his hazel eyes that my pulse fluttered. "You're the first person in a long time who's made me *glad* I got stuck with this job."

I tugged him to a stop and bobbed up on my toes to kiss him. He met me with the graze of his fingers into my hair, and for a moment I just reveled in the fact that I could do this now without any fears of ruining him, without tasting guilt on his lips.

Then thunder rumbled through the clouds overhead. Declan drew back with a concerned glance at the sky. "Maybe we should head back to the car."

We'd only backtracked a few steps when the first

raindrops started to fall. I picked up my pace, pulling my jacket tighter around me. It wasn't much protection as the drizzle picked up to a steady patter, cold water seeping into my hair and dappling my cheeks.

Another boom echoed down from above, and the clouds opened up with a total deluge. Rain poured down over us so thickly I could barely make out the path ahead. A yelp slipped from my throat. Declan grabbed my hand again, and we ran together, his lantern's light rippling over the rain, until the lamps along the highway beamed blearily through the downpour.

When we reached the car, Declan opened a back door and motioned me inside. I scrambled in, grateful to escape the flood. The rain drummed against the roof as Declan followed me with a thump of the closing door.

A shiver ran through me beneath my drenched clothes. Declan hugged me to him, but not much warmth penetrated the layers of soaked fabric covering both our bodies. He let go of me to lean between the front seats. "I'll get the engine running and turn on the heat."

I didn't know how much that was going to help unless he turned the interior into a sauna. As he fiddled with the controls, I peeled off my jacket. My skirt and blouse felt just as heavy and unpleasant against my skin. I hesitated, and then hauled my blouse over my head too.

Declan dropped back into the seat just as I'd tossed my blouse aside. His eyebrows rose, a teasing but still appreciative glint coming into his eyes.

"It's what you're supposed to do if you're, like, on the

verge of hypothermia or something," I said in my defense. "You dry off and warm up faster with the wet clothes off."

"That does actually make sense," he said, still sounding amused, and reached for the buttons on his own shirt, which was plastered to his slim frame.

By the time I'd kicked off my soggy shoes and wriggled out of my skirt, Declan had stripped down to his boxers. He'd left the overhead light off, but I could feel his attention on me, on the bare skin I'd uncovered, in the dim light that seeped through the windows from the car's running lights.

The air was still cool, only a thin trickle of warmth reaching us from the vents. I scooted across the seat and brushed his damp hair back from his forehead. He wrapped his arms around me. Without our soaked clothes in the way, the contact did heat me up quite a bit. In various ways.

"Better?" he asked by my ear in a voice so low it sent desire spiking through me.

"I don't know," I said, tracing my fingers down his side. "I think we've still got too many clothes on."

He laughed and tipped his head to seek out my mouth. We kissed hard and fast, carried on a wave of lust I clearly wasn't the only one feeling. I ran my hands over the compact muscle of his chest, and he dislodged my bra to cup my breast. One flick of his thumb over my nipple had me gasping.

I arched into his touch as he shifted his focus from one side to the other. Maybe he'd studied me as avidly as he did all those books of rules and records, because he seemed to know how to provoke the right reactions in me as well as if we'd done this a hundred times instead of only twice.

He kissed my shoulder and then the swell of my breast as he unhooked my bra completely. "I wouldn't give this up for anything," he murmured against my skin.

I wasn't sure he could really mean that, but I wasn't going to argue, especially not when his mouth had closed hot and hungry over my nipple. I sucked in a breath at the jolt of pleasure.

Declan tipped me back onto the seat, and I took the opportunity to wrench at his boxers. He helped me yank them off him and dropped them into the heap of wet clothes we were accumulating on the floor. Then he leaned in to claim my lips again. Fresh bliss rippled through me with each stroke of his hands across my chest, down my sides, over my thighs.

He hooked his fingers around the hem of my panties, and I lifted my hips to give him better access. A whimper escaped me as my core grazed his erection, and Declan let out a groan. He tossed my panties aside and teased his fingers over my clit with such precision the rush of pleasure made my hips jump all over again of their own accord.

When he eased his hand lower to trace over my slit, a different sort of wanting rose up in me—to be a full partner in this act, to take one small responsibility of the many weighing on him off his shoulders.

"Declan," I said, and had to swallow a moan as his fingers dipped inside me. "I— Can you teach me how to cast the protection spell? I really should know how to take care of myself, shouldn't I?"

Declan gazed down at me, and I wasn't sure what was sexier—the desire in his taut expression or the thought that after all the innocuous magic he'd taught me in his role as teacher's aide, he could now be my instructor in a much more intimate fashion.

"Of course," he said, his voice rough. "It's a simple Physicality technique. Whatever words fit best for you, you use them to conjure a thin barrier inside. You just want to picture it totally solid and covering you completely. There are other aspects that can make things less... messy afterward, and that sort of thing, but they're not essential."

I didn't have the patience for a full tutorial right now. "I'll stick to the basics," I said, and reached down to align my hand with his. Closing my eyes, I pictured that space inside me where he fit so well and murmured, "Protect," with a pulse of the magic in my chest.

The energy tingled through my arm and across my inner flesh. Declan held himself over my body, careful not to distract me, until I was sure the spell was finished. Then I clutched him close, and he kissed me with a ragged breath.

He swiveled his thumb over my clit until I was growling for more. His hand slid under my ass to lift me up to meet him. My feet bumped the far door, but I didn't give a shit. Not when he was sliding into me with such a perfect burn of bliss.

His patience had obviously worn thin too. He thrust

into me with an urgency I couldn't help echoing. I pulled his mouth back to mine, moaning as he plunged even deeper inside. The giddy burn spread from my core through my whole torso. I bucked up to meet him and cried out as the pleasure swept through me twice as potent as before. A tremor ran up my spine as I came apart.

Declan stiffened over me with the impact of his own release. Then he bowed his head, capturing my mouth for one more kiss. The rain rattled on above us, and there was barely room for us to cuddle on the narrow surface, but right then, there wasn't anything I'd have given up this moment for either.

CHAPTER THIRTEEN

Rory

When the blacksuits' car pulled into the university parking lot on Tuesday morning, it was the same driver as before. I studied him, as much as I could see beyond the back of his head, as I got in behind him.

"Are we doing the ceremony at the same place?" I asked as he gunned the engine.

"Yes," he said, flat and terse. Not the most talkative guy ever.

I trained even more attention on the neatly combed strands of his dun hair, rolling my general insight casting word onto my tongue. Attempting to peek inside the head of any blacksuit was risky. In their training, they must have learned all kinds of techniques against intrusions. Maybe this wasn't the smartest idea ever.

But this guy was clearly pretty low in the hierarchy if he was being given the role of chauffeur while the others set up the actual spell. I had a better chance of gleaning something from him than someone like Lillian. And Insight was my specialty. I'd like to think over the months I'd developed a fair bit of skill there.

I exhaled like a sigh and managed to work the casting word into the sound so faintly it shouldn't have been perceivable. "Franco." It was the only casting word I'd gotten in the habit of using that wasn't literally connected to the intent of the spell—my adoptive parents' last name, in honor of the value they'd instilled in me to care what went on in other people's heads.

As I spoke, I kept a tight rein on my magic. The blacksuit would definitely notice if I launched an obvious assault on his mental walls. Instead, I let the power that guided my awareness stretch out tentatively, testing the edges of the magic that formed a barrier around his mind.

He *did* have a solid wall up. No impressions slipped out to me in my initial feint. But my magic caught on a small weak point in that shield where his casting was a little thinner than elsewhere. I focused on that spot and let the energy I was extending push on it gently.

A few wavering images flickered through my consciousness: a stern face too blurry for me to recognize, a jab of frustration, and a whiff of the deeper anger I'd sensed during Sunday's ceremony. Then the guy shifted in his seat with a twitch as if he'd sensed something off, and I jerked my awareness back with a stutter of my pulse.

I hadn't been able to get a clear enough picture to know if the anger had anything to do with my mother's situation, but it definitely wasn't a *good* sign for calmer tempers among the blacksuits.

When we reached the field, it looked like the other blacksuits were just finishing their set-up. This hadn't been the same kind of rush job as on the weekend. Lillian nodded to me as I got out of the car, bending to place one more conducting piece.

Maggie was standing by a sapling near the edge of the field, her arms crossed loosely over her chest. I thought her eyes might have narrowed for a second when she saw me, but her expression warmed with her usual cheerful demeanor so quickly I wasn't sure I hadn't imagined it because of the uneasiness I'd been left with after our most recent conversation. She hustled over to give me a quick once-over with the lavender water.

Lillian straightened up and strode over to meet me just as Maggie was finishing. "We'll proceed the same way we did before," she said. "I have a couple more staff on hand to watch for any interference at the other end and diffuse that if it occurs. We just need you to take your spot on the center point again—"

"Lillian," I said quickly, before she could barrel on into the ceremony, "before we get started, there's something I wanted to talk to you about."

She frowned at me, shifting on her feet with her typical predatory grace. "We're not in the same rush as before, but the ideal window is still limited. Can't it wait for afterward?"

I steeled myself. "It won't take long. I just want your word that once you know approximately where my mother is, you'll bring me with you on the mission to get her free."

And I wanted that word given in front of all these witnesses, so it'd be awfully hard for her to go back on it.

Lillian blinked at me. "Rory—that wouldn't be standard procedure."

"How much of a standard can you have when barons aren't kidnapped every day—or even every decade? She's my mother. I want to be there. You'll be able to figure out her exact location faster if I can also help you with the spells nearby, won't you?"

I could tell from her expression that my last point was true. Her frown hadn't shifted, though. "It's likely to be a dangerous operation. Your mother will be heavily guarded. I can't in good conscience take you into a situation like that. Other than her, you're the only Bloodstone left."

I waved in the general direction of California. "Declan Ashgrave was allowed to come along on the mission to get *me* out of the joymancers' custody, even though he's the only Ashgrave you've got."

"You were being held in a much less secure fashion."

"You don't even know how my mother is being held yet." I gave her the most firm look I could summon. She might be some thirty years my elder and a high-ranking blacksuit, but I was the Bloodstone scion and, until my mother was back here, as close to a baron as they had. That authority had to be worth something. "I'm not insisting you take me into battle. I just want to be there and part of the discussion—to know what's happening, and to contribute if I can. I don't think that's too much to ask."

Her jaw worked. The gazes of the other blacksuits around the field were trained on us, which she could no doubt feel as well as I could. I thought I'd made a solid argument.

"I lived with joymancers for seventeen years," I added for good measure. "It might turn out I saw or heard things that'll end up helping us get her out."

Whether it was my last point that nudged her over the edge or she'd been on the verge of agreeing anyway, I wasn't sure, but Lillian's shoulders relaxed slightly. She gave a wry chuckle.

"Every time we talk, I see more of the Bloodstone in you. Your mother would have made the same argument in your position. All right—when we head south, you'll come with us. Now can we begin?"

"Yes. Thank you." I hurried over to my designated spot so I wouldn't annoy the blacksuits with any more delays. My sense of victory was tempered by Lillian's comment about my mother. Did I *want* to be like the woman who'd considered Malcolm's father a good friend?

I guessed I'd find that out once I got to meet her in the flesh... which shouldn't be much farther off now.

The grass squeaked under my shoes, still damp from last night's rain, but the clouds had finally broken. Mid-morning sun streamed over me. I turned my face to its warmth for a moment before readying myself by the central conducting piece. "Go ahead."

My body tensed slightly at the rising murmurs of

casting around me. The memory of the emotions that had trickled through me alongside the previous rush of magic was still fresh in my mind. Then the flood of energy hit me, sizzling through my body, and for a few seconds I couldn't think or remember much at all.

The edge of fury niggled at me again, but I focused my attention on the stream of magic flowing out of me to the southwest. The blacksuits were angry—fine. I'd committed to this course. Hopefully I'd be able to mitigate the worst of the violence if I was there alongside them planning the assault. If I didn't cooperate now, eventually they'd find a way to move forward without me.

The wave of energy swept me onward, even as it gnawed at my muscles. I was going to feel plenty of impact afterward; that much I could tell. I dragged air into my lungs and reached out toward the main area of our search. Where was that glimmer of a presence I'd known down to my bones was my mother? Where had the joymancers locked her away?

There. A hint of the impression grazed my senses. My heart thumped faster in anticipation, but this time I didn't let my nerves get the better of me. I stretched farther, urging the magic rushing through me to follow my lead, pointing it toward our goal.

I felt as if my mind yawned open between here and there, and then a fresh surge of outside magic slammed into me as the blacksuits caught on. I lost my breath, my sense of my body, all thought except the crackle of supernatural energy that consumed me. Somewhere in the midst of that furor, my mother's presence remained, like a faint but undeniable glow. I grasped onto it and tried to hold steady, steady, steady—

A blazing pain tore through my skull and echoed through my limbs. My legs gave. The blacksuits' magic wrenched out of me as I toppled to the ground.

My head smacked the grass. I winced and reached a wobbly arm to cradle it, my gaze rolling up to the sky.

Lillian reached my side a second later. She touched my head as if checking for obvious injuries, her expression a weird mix of elation and concern. I'd have liked to sit up to face her properly, but every muscle in my body ached with exhaustion. I'd take a little more time on the ground, thank you.

"Did it work?" I asked, my voice coming out strained. "Did you find her?"

Lillian nodded with a small smile. "You did wonderfully, Rory. We know exactly where to go. They have her in Sacramento. You'll have a chance to recover while we prepare our initial plan of action, but we should be able to leave before the end of the week."

CHAPTER FOURTEEN

Declan

I'd planned on touching base with Jude later—not right when I was heading off to a meeting of the pentacle of barons, in any case. But running into him on the third floor landing as I was heading down from my dorm was too convenient an opportunity to let pass.

Jude nodded hello to me without any hint of discomfort in his expression, which was a good sign. Hopefully it could be a brief conversation.

I held up my hand to stop him before he could continue on up. The staircase above and below us was empty, and I couldn't hear anyone out of sight, but just in case I pitched my voice low to avoid it carrying.

"Hey," I said. "Are we good? You seemed a little... unsettled when the bunch of us were talking in the lounge on Saturday. I didn't like keeping a secret from the rest of you—I spent most of that time trying to avoid having anything I needed to be secretive about in the first place."

"But she's just too irresistible, huh?" Jude's smile was more amused than anything else. "Don't beat yourself up, Mr. By-The-Books. It just caught me by surprise. She's certainly united the pentacle of scions, hasn't she?"

To the extent that it might be difficult to disengage ourselves from her when we needed to. But I wasn't going to let myself worry about that now—I'd made my decision. "Just so you know, she was always upfront with me that she was seeing you. She never diminished her relationship with you in any way."

"I wasn't nervous about that. She's got at least ten times as much caring and compassion in her than any fearmancer I know. I think there's plenty to go around between the four of us."

That should have been enough to satisfy me, but I couldn't shake the niggling sense that *something* more than surprise had affected him during the meeting. I might never use insight on my fellow scions without permission, but when you studied the art as much as I had, you developed a knack for reading people without magic too, once you saw certain patterns over and over. Jude had wanted to get out of that conversation—it had unnerved him somehow.

"If there's anything else bothering you, you know you can talk to me, right?" I said. "If your father has been hassling you the way Connar's parents have him—or laying into you like Malcolm's—"

Jude cut me off with a jerky shake of his head. "Are you offering as a friend or as one scion to another?" he asked, his gaze sharpening.

I wasn't sure how to answer that. "As far as I'm concerned, they're part of the same thing. I might have one foot in the door as baron, but our pentacle is still my first priority. As colleagues and as friends."

Jude's smile tightened. He shrugged and moved to saunter past me. "Well, you don't need to worry about me either. No projects here for you to fix."

The matter didn't feel entirely settled, but I didn't think he'd appreciate me chasing after him—and I didn't really have time to right now anyway. I tabled it in my mind as a potential issue to follow up on later and hurried on down the stairs.

I might have appreciated the drive on the warm and sunny September day more if I hadn't been so apprehensive of what might be waiting for me at the Fortress of the Pentacle. It was our first official meeting since Rory had foiled the older barons' plans and been absolved of the murder charge. Because it was an official meeting, my aunt Ambrosia would almost certainly be making the trip to lord over the Ashgrave point on the table with her limited authority as regent for the last bit of time she had in that role.

The meetings of the barony were rarely pleasant, and this one seemed likely to be even less so than usual.

I soaked in a last bit of sunshine on the short walk from the parking lot to the ominous stone presence of the Fortress and then stepped into the cool halls. My feet rapped against the polished floor too loudly as I made my way to the meeting room. A couple of voices trickled out —Julian Nightwood's and Marguerite Stormhurst's. Theirs had been the only other cars in the lot so far.

They trailed off in their conversation as I came in, Baron Nightwood watching me with cool consideration and Baron Stormhurst with a slight edge of hostility. I took my seat at the Ashgrave point on the round table with its pentacle carving.

"No need for the other chair," Nightwood said with a glance toward the second seat at my end. "We neglected to mention this meeting to your aunt. Her presence is barely even necessary as a formality at this point."

I'd have celebrated her absence if I hadn't distrusted the man who'd arranged it so much. "Was there any particular reason for that call?" I said evenly.

He folded his hands on his table, his demeanor even more imperious than I'd seen Malcolm manage, for all the Nightwood scion looked like a younger version of his father. "We have matters to discuss that require even more discretion than usual."

"So, where the hell is Killbrook?" Baron Stormhurst muttered, flexing her sinewy shoulders as she braced her elbows on the table.

Jude's father arrived with just a minute to spare, rubbing his narrow jaw. Giving off his usual harried vibe, he dropped into his chair without bothering to remove his jacket and scanned the table. "Let's get started, then. What's this momentous news, Nightwood?"

Obviously Baron Nightwood had already tipped the

others off a little more than he'd bothered to inform me. I leaned back in my chair at a casual angle, not wanting to show my tension.

Nightwood cleared his throat and glanced at each of us in turn. In that instant, I couldn't help wondering what the pentacle of barons would have been like if my mother and Rory's hadn't been torn from it, if Connar's mother had never wrenched the position from his uncle. Like I'd told Rory, the Barons Nightwood and Bloodstone had been allies—and long-time friends. The original Baron Stormhurst had grown up with them. And maybe all that upheaval had made Baron Killbrook more withdrawn than he'd been before.

My mother might never have totally fit in, but the other four of them might have made a much tighter group than we had now. The older barons were willing to scheme together so they could each reach their own ends, some of which they shared, but I never got the impression they *liked* each other all that much.

I sure as hell hoped our generation wouldn't end up in the same position once we all reached the table.

Nightwood's mouth set in a thin line that was almost a smile. "I've been informed by a high ranking member of the blacksuits that Althea Bloodstone is still alive and has most likely been in joymancer custody for the past seventeen years. They're already planning an operation to retrieve her as soon as possible."

I made my eyes widen as if this was news to me, the way it should have been if Rory had kept the subject secret as the blacksuits would have wanted. Baron Stormhurst just stared at Nightwood for a few beats. Killbrook's lips parted in shock. Then he started to chuckle.

"My God. All this time, and the queen of Bloodstone rises up from the dead. I should have known she'd be capable of a maneuver like that."

"Are they completely sure?" Stormhurst asked, but the urgency in her voice sounded more eager than wary.

"My source waited until they were certain before she passed the word on to me, to avoid the chaos that would result if they made an announcement like that only to have to retract it." Nightwood's lips curled a little farther. He was definitely smiling now. "We'll have to wait and see what state she's in after what the joymancers have put her through—but Althea's made of strong stuff. I expect our problems with the Bloodstone point on the pentacle have come to an end."

He assumed that whatever move they'd wanted to bully—or outright force—Rory into supporting, her mother would be immediately on board with. A chill twisted through my gut.

Rory had asked me how her mother fit in with the pentacle—what she'd believed, how she might have behaved. Maybe I could give her more of an answer if I asked my questions carefully enough.

"Do you think she'll be able to bring her daughter in line?" I asked, as if that was a totally reasonable thing to want.

"She's certainly not going to tolerate any joymancerinfluenced attitudes," Killbrook said with another rough chuckle.

"Or Nary-sympathizing." Nightwood lifted his head haughtily. "She knows their proper place."

That definitely wasn't encouraging. Rory might not be all that keen on the joymancers as a group anymore, but she'd still picked up a lot of her parents' gentler perspective —a perspective no one could have mistaken for normal fearmancer ideals. I couldn't imagine Baron Bloodstone would feel anything but rage toward her long-time captors after her ordeal, and that feeling might extend to anyone who criticized the fearmancer approach.

Of course, she also hadn't seen her daughter in nearly two decades and might have spent that time assuming the girl was dead. Was there any chance maternal affection would override the political side of things?

I kept my tone as mild as before. "Of course, she might be rather upset when she finds out what her daughter has been through, between the murder charge and the various incidents at school."

Nightwood waved his hand dismissively. "The girl was broken in. She had a fair hearing. There's nothing worthy of dispute there."

There would be if it came out that the three figures sitting at the table with me had orchestrated most of Rory's troubles. But before I could find another angle from which to nudge for more information, Stormhurst spun on Killbrook.

"What the hell is the matter with *your* heir?" she

demanded in her usual blunt manner. "Word is going around that he made a show of leaving the Killbrook properties—that he's gone off and taken an apartment on his own?"

What? *That* news was a total surprise. Jude hadn't mentioned a thing to any of us scions about it, as far as I knew.

His father shrugged stiffly. "Young men want to stretch their independence. He's always been rather obstinate. I'll give him a chance to get the impulse out of his system before I rein him in."

Stormhurst let out a huff. "Be sure you don't leave it too long, or it'll reflect badly on the Killbrooks as a whole. Can't expect much from a baron-to-be who doesn't even respect his own family."

It was Killbrook's turn to smile. "Soon he won't be my only heir. My family will have options."

Was that what had made Jude edgy—had his father already threatened to disown him as scion? Fucking hell, he should have told us if that was the case. There had to be something we could do to settle the matter in his favor. Jude might be prickly at certain times and careless at others, but he got his act together when it counted. He'd proven that with Rory more than once, not that his father would have seen that as a mark in his favor.

I'd known they'd never really gotten along, but I'd had no idea their relationship had fractured to such an extreme.

"An additional heir is an excellent point of leverage

among other things," Nightwood said. His gaze slid to me, and I tensed under his scrutiny while keeping up the appearance of nonchalance as well as I could. "The talk of siblings reminds me. We made an executive decision that didn't require full votes, Ashgrave."

I cocked my head, suppressing the thump of my pulse. "A decision about what?"

Killbrook focused on me, clearly glad that he was no longer the center of attention. His eyes narrowed. "You stepped down as teacher's aide. There's no more conflict of interest. No reason your brother and secondary scion should be getting his education from mages overseas whom we can barely monitor."

My stomach flipped. Oh, no. They hadn't—

They had. Nightwood looked so satisfied I wanted to lean across the table and punch him so hard I knocked the smirk off his face. I caught my hands before they could even clench.

"We've summoned Noah Ashgrave to Bloodstone University," he said. "He's had plenty of international broadening as it is. I'm sure it'll be a relief for you to have your brother back at home with you."

Back at home where the other barons could make him a target of their schemes so much easier. Where they could use him to try to manipulate me. I swallowed hard, fighting down both my temper and a wave of nerves.

It'd been hard enough to feel Noah was totally safe with an ocean between him and the figures in front of me. They hadn't chosen this moment to change the power balance for no reason. They meant to threaten him any way they could to keep me in line.

And I had to pretend I didn't know that. Had to pretend it was a relief and not a threat.

I forced myself to smile. "It will," I said. "How very considerate of you."

CHAPTER FIFTEEN

Rory

Lillian might have agreed to let me come along to California, but I didn't trust her and her blacksuit colleagues to actually keep me in the loop when it came to all their plans. So after my classes the next day, I holed up in the library grabbing all the books I could on illusionary techniques.

At the Nightwood home, Declan had cast a spell on me that made me difficult to see even when I was moving around on open ground. If I could manage to pull something like that off on myself, I might be able to overhear a whole lot more than the blacksuits would want me to know.

When I found a volume of practical magical strategies that explained the concept in simple terms, it used pretty much the same phrasing Declan had—the idea was to reflect aspects of your surroundings onto your body so you blended in with them. It was easier to avoid detection if you stood still or only moved slowly, and if your environment didn't include too many distinctive details. I'd just have to hope for plain hotel decor wherever we ended up staying.

My first couple attempts at casting the spell didn't get me very far, but as I refined my focus, I was able to create a strong enough illusion on my arm that it blended into the bookshelves I waved it in front of—with some rippling, sure, because a library was hardly an ideal setting for the illusion, but effective enough that I had to smile.

I was just turning back to the book to see if it'd mention any other techniques I might find useful when my phone rang. I dug it out of my purse before the sound could disturb the other library-goers any more than it already had.

It was Lillian. My heart skipped a beat as I brought the phone to my ear. She wasn't going to back out of our agreement, was she?

"Hey," I said, as calmly as I could. "What's the news?"

"We're set to fly out tomorrow," she said. "The tickets and hotel rooms are all arranged—I'll come by myself to pick you up for the drive to the airport at nine in the morning. Unless you've changed your mind about joining us?"

"No," I said quickly with a rush of relief. "I still want to be as much a part of the operation as I can be."

"Your presence will definitely make the final locating spells easier, as you suggested. We'll see how you can fit into the rest." She let out a breath. "Can you pass on the pick-up time to your colleague Mr. Nightwood as well?"

I froze. "Mr. Nightwood?"

"Yes, it doesn't make any sense to force him to make the trip separately. Oh, and we shouldn't be there for more than a few days, so no need to pack very much. I'll see you then."

She hung up before I could ask her why the hell Malcolm would be making the trip at all. I stared at my phone for a second, my jaw tensing. I'd just have to ask "Mr. Nightwood" myself. Although I could make a pretty good guess.

We need to talk, I texted him. *Where are you right now?*

It took a few minutes before he answered, during which I tried and failed to go back to concentrating on my research books. Finally, my phone pinged with an alert.

Just finishing up an evening run. We'll be back at A. Hall in a few minutes, if this is so urgent.

I left my books and headed out of Ashgrave Hall so I could meet him—and whoever he was with—right away. Coming around the building, I spotted Malcolm and Connar walking briskly across the field on their way up from the lake. They weren't running anymore, but the damp patches on their uncharacteristically casual T-shirts showed they'd had a decent workout before this cool down.

The definition of their well-muscled chests—Connar's a little broader, but Malcolm's very fine in its own right—showed even in the fading evening light. They were certainly easy on the eyes. I'd have been able to appreciate the sight more if I hadn't been so irritated with Malcolm, a feeling that only sharpened when he shot his usual cocky grin my way.

I strode over to meet them partway across the field, not really wanting to have this conversation in earshot of the dorms. As I came up on them, Malcolm's familiar bounded across the grass to join us. The wolf bowed his head down with a swish of his tail and an eager gleam in his eyes, asking if I was going to play too.

"Maybe later," I told Shadow, but irritated or not, I couldn't resist bending down to give his ears a scratch.

"What's the emergency, Glinda?" Malcolm asked, but his tone was only lightly teasing, not mocking the way it would have been a couple months ago.

Connar watched the two of us a little cautiously, but he didn't continue on toward the hall. Maybe he thought I might still need a little protection from his friend. I didn't mind *him* hearing this argument.

I gave Malcolm a pointed look. "What made you think inviting yourself along on my mother's rescue operation was a good idea?"

He chuckled. "The blacksuits spilled the beans, did they? After the last stunt they pulled, I'd have thought you'd appreciate a little backup surrounded by a bunch of them."

Maybe I would have—but Malcolm wouldn't have been my first choice for that backup. And that wasn't the point.

"I get that you're trying to make up for what an asshole you were before," I said, "but you *really* have to get over the whole impulse to treat me like a damsel in distress. I've got no problem asking for help if I think I need it. I *don't* need a volunteer bodyguard stepping in at every slight hint of danger. I'm supposed to be holding my own as a scion, remember?"

The cockiness in his expression faltered. "Rory, that wasn't really—" He sighed and rubbed his hand over his face. "Okay, I can see how springing it on you like that wasn't the best idea. And I think you'll be better off with someone who'll have your back right there with you, *if* you need it. But honestly, I mostly wanted to go for my own peace of mind. After what my dad already put you through, it'd drive me crazy knowing you're off there in a situation like that and I have no idea whether you're okay."

"Oh." I hesitated, trying to decide how to respond to that. After all the ups and downs with Malcolm, it was still a little hard to wrap my head around the idea that he cared that much about what happened to me. "All right. As long as you're not planning on leaping to my defense before there's anything really to defend me from. You could have talked to me about it."

He shrugged with a sheepish smile. "I had a feeling it'd be better to ask forgiveness rather than permission."

Connar glanced at Malcolm with a frown. "Is your dad going to be pissed off all over again about you going with Rory?"

Malcolm grimaced. "I got *his* permission first. Spun a story about how I could keep an eye out and report back to him anything I thought he'd want to know. He doesn't really trust anyone, so he was happy to have eyes there other than his blacksuit lackeys."

"Well, the main blacksuit lackey is picking us up tomorrow morning at nine," I told him. "She wanted me to pass the message on."

"Got it." He snapped his fingers for his familiar to trot over and rubbed the wolf's chin. "I'd better take Shadow on a longer walk then—get in as much familiar time as possible before the separation. I'll see you in the morning."

I hadn't even thought about the discomfort of leaving his familiar behind—but of course he could hardly bring a wolf on a plane. He must have thought that discomfort wouldn't be anywhere near as bad as what he'd feel staying here while I was across the country.

"You're going already," Connar said as the Nightwood scion headed off. He didn't look all that comfortable with the idea either. "I didn't realize they'd move that fast."

"I think the blacksuit who was friends with my mother feels pretty guilty about assuming she was dead all this time. She wants to make up for that ASAP."

"That makes sense." He shifted toward me and then wavered for a moment. "Do you have any plans for tonight?"

I shook my head. "Other than packing, which shouldn't take more than a few minutes, not really. What did you have in mind?"

He ducked his head to give me a quick kiss. "Wait here while I get showered off, and I'll show you."

Summer hadn't left completely. The evening breeze carried a lingering warmth and the smell of the freshly mown grass to me as I waited. Connar loped around Ashgrave Hall less than ten minutes later, his chestnut-brown hair still damp from a hasty shower and his impressive physique back in the standard dress shirt and slacks. He was carrying a bag that he hefted as he approached me.

"I'm guessing you haven't eaten dinner yet."

No, I'd been too absorbed in my library research to think about that. Now, with the delicious savory yet buttery scent that drifted from the bag, my stomach grumbled loud enough that he must have heard it too.

"I got a little distracted," I said.

"It's a good thing I have enough for two, then."

He took my hand and headed for the forest at the far side of the field. It didn't take long for me to figure out his planned destination. We passed the primary ward for the campus Shifting Grounds, which he activated with a couple of intoned words, and then wandered on to the clearing where he'd shown me his dragon form... Had that really been less than two months ago?

We hunkered down on the grass, the trees sheltering us from all but a hint of the breeze and crickets chirping as if to welcome the stars starting to gleam overhead. Connar drew a couple of small chicken pies and forks from the bag and offered me one of each. We leaned against neighboring pines as we dug into our dinner.

"It'll be a pretty big change, having your mother back," the Stormhurst scion remarked between bites. A shadow of concern passed over his face when he looked at me. "You've never really known her."

"No. So I guess we'll just have to see how that goes." I jabbed at a piece of chicken coated in creamy sauce. "Given what I've seen of the baron families so far, I'm going to proceed with caution."

"That… seems like a good idea." He paused. "At least she'll have to be more careful with you than if she had another heir."

I nearly choked on a startled laugh at all the awful implications that came with that comment. "Small mercies?" Considering how his parents had treated him and his brother, I could see why his mind would go there.

He met my gaze again, his light blue eyes utterly serious. "I just want you to know that if anything goes wrong with her, if you're not sure how to handle her expectations or anything like that, you can turn to me. To any of us scions, I'd imagine. We all know what it's like, but you've never had to deal with those kinds of pressures before."

"Well, I've dealt with all of *your* parents, so at least I can hope she won't be significantly worse than that," I said wryly.

He gave me a half-smile. "There is that. But it's different when it's coming from within your own family."

Of course it was. As delicious as the meal he'd brought me was, it was settling heavy in my stomach with this conversation.

Some of that uneasiness must have shown in my expression, because Connar's immediately turned regretful.

"Sorry. I didn't want to stress you out before you even have her back. It's amazing the blacksuits were able to locate her at all." His smile turned sweeter. "I like what we have now, the way we all relate to each other. Maybe it's partly selfish, but I'm not looking forward to seeing how that might be thrown off."

"Neither am I," I admitted. "And it does help, knowing I have you and the other guys for support. At the moment, it's hard for me to think much past getting her out of the joymancers' hands. I have no idea what state she'll be in or how she'll handle the return." Hell, she might not even be fit to resume her role as baron, depending on how badly the joymancers had treated her. They'd kept her locked up for *some* reason, and presumably it wasn't anything joyful.

"Let's not think about it at all for the rest of the night, then," Connar suggested.

I set aside the nearly empty pie dish and tipped my head back against the tree trunk. "I like this spot, but isn't it kind of abusing your Shifting Grounds privileges to use them for things other than shifting?"

A hint of mischief came into Connar's eyes. "We could add shifting to the program if you'd like. There's actually…" He looked down at his hands and then back at me. "I can think of something that might really take your mind off tomorrow and everything after."

I raised my eyebrows at him. "Don't tell me you've learned how to shift into something even more amazing than a dragon."

He laughed. "No, I think one mythological form is enough for me. But *while* I'm a dragon… I think you could fly with me. I'm pretty sure I'm strong enough to carry you."

My breath caught a little just at the thought. "Are you sure? I wouldn't want to accidentally hurt you."

"If I feel there's any danger of that, I'll stop," he said. "Do you want to give it a try?"

He looked so adorably and shyly enthusiastic that it'd have been difficult for me to say no even if the idea hadn't given me a huge thrill. I stood up. "Sure. Why not? I'll definitely have trouble thinking about anything else in the middle of that."

Connar beamed at me with the smile that had first made me fall for him. He got up too, reaching for the buttons on his shirt so he could strip it off. He'd told me before that he found it easiest to shift while naked, although last time he'd felt awkward enough about that to leave his boxers on.

He did the same this time, but he walked into the middle of the clearing without any sign of hesitation. When he bent down toward the grass, my pulse sped up in anticipation.

The shift came over him gradually and then so quickly it seemed over in an instant. His back hunched, his skin darkened with a rippling of scales, his jaw stretched, and suddenly his form was expanding and reshaping itself at the same time, limbs and muscles aligning in their new order, wings sprouting from his now-massive back and a tail lashing behind him.

He didn't exactly match the dragons of my childhood

books, but he probably couldn't have. The being in front of me looked much more *real*, an amalgamation of lizard and dinosaur and something almost equine, eyes the same pale blue blinking at me from within their frame of glossy scales.

Connar bent his new expanded form as low to the ground as it would go, which left the dragon's back at about my chin height. He tucked his wings close. As I walked up to him, he shifted one of his forelegs back so I could use it as a sort of stepladder.

"You're sure?" I said again.

He nodded, watching me avidly. I clambered up as carefully as I could, awe washing through me at the warmth that emanated through those smooth scales. It took me a minute to settle myself by his shoulder blades in a position that felt secure. I lowered myself against his neck, wrapping my arms around as far as they would go, my knees tensed against his sides.

"Okay, I'm ready."

The muscles in his back shifted against my thighs. He stood and took a few swift steps, testing my balance. When I stayed in place, he sprang up with an unfurling of his wings.

I completely lost my breath in that first moment. The wind rushed past me and the ground fell away beneath us, and nothing existed except the deepening night and me and the dragon that was both Connar and not. The expansive wings on either side of me flapped, carrying us higher.

Before, he'd only skimmed the ground within the clearing. He must have decided it was safe to soar a little above the treetops in the dusk. The dark green shapes slipped by beneath us in a blur. I clung to him even more tightly, the musky smoky smell that always lingered on Connar's skin filling my nose.

Going very far or staying up there very long would have been too much of a risk, I knew. I relished every second as he circled over the edge of the lake and then veered back toward the clearing. A twinge of disappointment rippled through me as he came back to earth. Of course, who knew how much carrying me had tired him out on top of holding the shift.

I scrambled off him without much grace and nearly fell on my ass. Connar shifted back into his human form so quickly he grasped my hand before I'd quite finished catching my balance. He grinned at me, and I grinned right back at him, still giddy from the flight.

"That was amazing," I said. "You're okay?"

"Wonderful," he said. "I've never— You're the first person I've ever tried that with."

I'd gotten the impression that might be true from the way he'd offered, but his acknowledgment sent a flush of happiness through me. "It was an honor."

"For me as much as you. You have no idea how much it means to me that I can share every part of who I am with you, Rory." He tugged me closer into a tight embrace and kissed my cheek. His voice dipped. "I love you. I don't want you leaving tomorrow without knowing that."

My heart fluttered. I squeezed him back with all my strength, emotion swelling in my throat. "I love you too," I said. "Every part of you."

He sucked in a breath, and then he was kissing me on the mouth, so hard I lost my breath all over again. My hands roamed over his nearly naked body, so solid and so hot even in the cooling night air.

We ended up sinking onto the grass, me straddling his lap. A gasp slipped out of me at the sensation of that even harder and hotter part of him pressing between my legs through the layers of fabric. But Connar didn't rush things. He let his kisses turn slow and tender, stretching out each one until they left me quivering. At the same time, he rested his hand on my hip and gently rocked me against him. It didn't take long before I was burning with the need for more.

"There's one part of you I'd *especially* like to experience right now," I mumbled against his lips, and he chuckled, sounding breathless himself. He eased up my dress, and I pushed myself higher so he could help me out of my panties. With a murmur, I repeated the spell Declan had taught me. Then I delved inside his boxers to free Connar's rigid cock. Just the feel of it in my hand brought a hungry sound into my throat.

I kissed him again, with all the tenderness he'd offered me, and sank down onto him.

A whimper spilled from my lips at the fullness of him inside me. He braced one hand against the ground to hold us steady while the other stroked over my breasts. We kissed harder, faster, as I rocked over him, urging him deeper. Soon I couldn't do much more than moan with the pleasure flooding my core.

As my thighs started to tremble, Connar returned his

hand to my hip, lending his strength to my rhythm. As we sped up together, he groaned. Fresh bliss blazed through me with each thrust up into me. My lips collided with his one last time just before I shattered. Connar clutched my hip as he came with me.

He caught me, tipping back so I could lie over him in the ecstatic afterglow. I tucked my head under his chin, boneless and sated, and he caressed my hair.

"You can ride me any time you want," he said with a smile in his voice.

I giggled and nuzzled his chest. "Believe me, I'll take you up on that offer."

As long as I returned from California in one piece.

CHAPTER SIXTEEN

Rory

The blacksuits obviously had a certain sense of discretion concerning our mission. I'd half expected a stretch limo to be waiting for us at the Sacramento airport to take us to our hotel, but instead we piled into a series of regular cabs. To Malcolm's obvious chagrin, I ended up in one with Lillian and Maggie rather than him.

"The hotel will be very comfortable," Lillian assured me, as if she thought I might mind the method of transportation.

Her assistant, who was sitting between us, gave me a look I couldn't read. "I'm sure you wouldn't want anything but the best, after all."

If that was intended as some kind of jab, I didn't follow it. Lillian didn't remark on it, though, so maybe it wasn't such an odd comment. It *might* sound odd if I emphasized how little I cared about fancy accommodations.

I gazed out the window at the California landscape we were cruising past. Even with the windows closed, I could taste the warm dry air. My stomach tightened. No matter where I'd been born, no matter what legacy awaited me, I wasn't sure anywhere but this state would ever feel completely like home.

Deborah shifted in her perch beneath my hair at the back of my neck. I'd smuggled her along on the airplane without mentioning her presence to any of the blacksuits. Malcolm had needed to leave his familiar behind, but there was no way I was going to risk the unsettling sensation of being thousands of miles apart from mine for who knew exactly how many days.

She hadn't said anything since we'd left Blood U, because we'd been in the company of blacksuits the whole time and she wouldn't want to risk revealing the unexpected aspect of our connection, but I suspected she had to feel some sort of homecoming too. As far as I knew, she'd lived in California her entire life, which'd been a heck of a lot longer than mine so far.

Of course, it was hard to feel totally at peace when I knew the company I'd arrived with was already making violent plans.

"It'll take us some time to confirm we have an appropriate location for the next locating spell and get it set up," Lillian said, flicking through information on her phone's screen. "You should take that time to relax and enjoy the hotel so you're calm and centered for the ceremony. Just keep your phone on you and don't wander too far."

"I don't think that'll be a problem." After the long drive to the airport and the longer flight after that, I was looking forward to crashing on my hotel bed for at least a little while.

"Hopefully we won't run into any of the problems we had with the first locating spell, now that we're so much closer to the joymancers," Maggie said. "It'd be a lot more of a setback if we had to delay here—and possibly put the whole operation in danger."

Her tone stayed mild, but Lillian shot her a curious look that told me she hadn't expected her assistant to be worrying along those lines. My back prickled. I suspected the supposedly stray comment was meant as a warning to me.

Especially with Lillian's next remark. "We should be able to catch any joymancer interference and neutralize it before it can affect our casting *because* we're so much closer now," she said confidently.

In other words, if the spell got screwed up, it'd be much more obvious I was to blame. Well, it was a good thing I didn't have any intention of throwing it off, then.

"I'm glad to hear that," I said, ignoring Maggie's insinuation. She couldn't *know* that the first failure had been my fault, and I sure as hell wasn't going to confirm it for her. "It takes enough out of me just doing it once."

Lillian smiled at me—the first truly warm smile I'd seen from her in a while. "We really do appreciate how much you've given yourself over to the process, and I know your mother will be grateful for your efforts too, when I can tell her about them. Thankfully the locating spell here should be much less of a strain because we're searching across a much smaller distance, much closer by."

That really was a relief. "I'm *very* glad to hear that," I said with a little laugh, and even Maggie smiled. Maybe she had just been expressing a general worry, not aiming her remark at me? The longer I spent around her, the less I felt I really knew about her.

But since she was only a blacksuit's assistant and not even a blacksuit herself, I didn't have to care what she thought of me as long as Lillian was happy.

The taxi pulled up in front of a broad white building with a huge wall of windows around the front entrance. Oh, yeah, that looked a lot more posh than our transportation had been.

Lillian ushered us into the lobby with its leather seating and tall potted plants. She handled most of the conversation with the staff at the front desk while I gazed around. Off at the back of the lobby, a couple of hallways branched off with a sign in between them, arrows indicating which direction you wanted to head in for which feature. Business center, pool, sauna, spa, exercise room… arcade? My lips twitched. I'd have to check that out if I got the chance.

Lillian had produced fake IDs for all of us including me, since obviously I couldn't go waltzing into joymancer territory declaring myself a Bloodstone. I signed a fake signature on the paper the concierge nudged toward me, and a bellhop came around to collect our bags. The number of the keycard I was handed didn't mean much to me until we got into the elevator and I realized we were going all the way to the top floor.

We'd gotten the penthouse suites. Apparently the blacksuits were as flush with cash as most of the fearmancer families appeared to be.

Lillian and Maggie's room was to the left of the elevators, and mine was to the right. Lillian gave me a brisk nod as they set off. I ambled down the hall with its few doors to the one that held my number.

The room on the other side wasn't exactly luxurious in the way the Bloodstone manor was, but everything about it screamed modern sophistication. I had a balcony with a sweeping city view, a huge soaker bathtub, and a king-sized bed that gave me more space to stretch out than the one I was used to in my dorm.

I left my suitcase by the foot of the bed and flopped onto the covers. Deborah scrambled off and came to crouch by my hand.

Well, they certainly don't skimp, do they? she said in her dry voice.

"At least I can sleep between soft sheets while I worry about impending catastrophes," I muttered, and burrowed my face into the duvet.

Your plan used to be that you'd escape back here when you had the chance. You could get away from the villains now. The Conclave's headquarters aren't far from Sacramento and these people aren't expecting you to make a run for it.

My entire body balked at the idea. "That was before," I said. "I didn't see the way I could help change things without anyone getting hurt. And people who don't deserve it would almost definitely get hurt if I sent the joymancers off to Villain Academy. Not that I have any more idea how to dismantle the wards defending it than I did before."

Deborah made a humming sound in my head. *I still think you'd be better off on the joymancer side of things. I could tell them how well you've handled yourself—they could use their version of insight on me to see you haven't given over to fearmancer ideals. Surely they wouldn't need more proof than that.*

"Well, we're not going to find out."

My familiar dropped the subject, but I still couldn't relax, even with the extra comfy bed. I squirmed onto one side and then the other, closed my eyes and then gazed out the window, but a thread of restlessness kept running through my chest. Finally I pushed myself upright.

"Will you be okay in here on your own for a little while?" I asked. "I'm going to check out the hotel facilities. I'll bring you some food when I get back."

I'll be just fine, Deborah said, tucking herself out of sight under one of the pillows. *I could use a nap.*

Lucky for her that she could manage to take one. Rolling my shoulders to try to release some of the built-up tension, I left the room and headed back to the elevator.

In less than a minute, I'd arrived back in the lobby. Right where Malcolm Nightwood happened to be standing, frowning at his surroundings. Or maybe at the number of Naries occupying them.

He raised his head with a hint of a smirk when he saw

me. "There you are. I didn't figure they could have lost you."

"If you wanted to know where I was, you could have texted me," I pointed out, and brushed past him.

He sauntered after me to the back of the lobby. "Where are you off to, Glinda? Going to take a swim?"

The comment and the slight dip of his voice made me remember the very interesting swim I'd taken in the campus lake at the same time as him—when we'd teased each other with magical currents of water to total distraction. A flicker of heat shot through me, but I willed it away.

"I was going to check out the arcade, actually. It's been a long time since I've played at one of those."

There'd been an old one down at the beach I'd sometimes gone to with my parents—the joymancer ones—when I was a kid. I'd never really thought about it until now, but… we'd stopped making those little trips right before I'd turned fifteen. Right before they'd needed to start worrying about whether I'd come into my fearmancer magic.

At the time, they'd talked about me growing out of the beach-side activities, and I'd accepted that because I had started to get a little bored of the strip. But maybe they'd just been nervous about having me a greater distance from whatever support systems they'd been able to count on back in the city.

I shook those thoughts away too. What my parents had or hadn't thought, I'd never know, because they were gone. Slaughtered by the same people who'd brought me here. I had to focus on doing what I could to reduce how many more people might die while we were here.

Which I'd be able to focus on better once I burned off some of this restlessness.

"An arcade," Malcolm repeated, his forehead furrowing.

I blinked at him. "Yeah, you know… Video games in cabinet-like consoles you can pop coins into to play. Don't tell me you've somehow completely missed out on them?"

He made a face at me. "If it's a standard Nary form of entertainment, there's a good chance my parents would have felt it beneath us. I've never happened across one on my own."

I guessed that was believable. The industry had been dying out now that just about everyone had game consoles at home.

I waved for him to follow me. "Come on, then. I'll show you what you've been missing. If you don't mind lowering yourself to my level."

"It'd take more than video games to ruin my opinion of you," Malcolm said wryly.

It looked as if the hotel's arcade might be on the verge of dying too. It definitely could have used some life support. Maybe fifteen consoles stood along the walls of the small dim room at the end of the hall, and a third of them had *Out Of Order* signs taped to their screens. The hotel must only keep the room open for the occasional visitors with younger kids. But I still spotted a few old favorites, and it looked as if they were set up to be free, no coins required.

I tugged Malcolm over to the Street Fighter unit. "Here we go. Let's see how quickly I can kick your ass in digital form."

Malcolm guffawed with mock indignance, which quickly turned into actual exasperation when I dealt a match-finishing blow to his character within less than a minute of starting the fight. He glowered at the knob and buttons in front of him. "I've played a newer version of this game, but with a proper controller. A magical battle would be better use of our skills, you know."

"Yeah, but for once I can challenge you at something where you don't have years more experience than I do." I elbowed him. "Or are you afraid to find out I'll beat you even faster the second time?"

It was way too easy to provoke him through pride. Malcolm bent over the controls again, his gaze flicking between his hands and mine and the screen, watching my technique as much as coming up with his own. This match, he got in a few good strikes before I pummeled him to the ground.

"Damn," he muttered. "Apparently I should be glad that your aggressive streak seems to be restricted to animated characters."

I laughed, my spirits already lighter. "I'll give you a few more rematches to catch up. It's only fair. You did the same for me, didn't you?"

He shot me a look as if to check whether I'd said that last bit with any bitterness, but I wasn't here to think about our history. We could goof around for a bit and have fun without the past hanging over us the way it so often did, couldn't we?

After a few more rounds and a couple of character switches, the Nightwood scion was giving me more of a challenge, but I was still crushing him in the end. I glanced around for something else to try before he got too beaten down.

"Maybe racing is more your speed than physical combat?" I suggested, nodding to the Mario Kart cabinet with its two steering wheels farther into the room.

Malcolm cracked his knuckles. "It'd better be."

The controls mustn't have been that different from what he was used to, or else it was simply that steering was more a matter of reflexes than remembering specific combos. His kart zipped ahead of me before I'd even warmed up. I let out a yelp of dismay and tore after him, grabbing a bonus that let me lob a bomb at him.

"Oh no, you don't," he said with a grin. His kart spun, but he splattered digital ink at my screen a few seconds later.

By the time we'd zipped around the track a few times, always neck and neck, we were both laughing between crows of victory as we took our turns in the lead. Malcolm edged ahead just in time to soar across the finish line.

"I hope you're not a sore loser," he said with an arch of his eyebrows.

"Nah. It's a lot more fun when you're actually giving me a challenge." I smirked right back at him and took another glance around. "Ah ha. You need the full range of experiences, since who knows if you'll ever be in an arcade again. Ever play Dance Dance Revolution?"

"I've *heard* of it. I grew up with fearmancers, not in a hole in the ground. But I don't play video games to *dance*."

"You do now," I informed him, and hauled him over to the platforms. "It's almost like spellcasting, you know. Follow the steps, stay focused, link up elements for a stronger effect… And it's a decent workout too."

He looked skeptical, but he climbed onto the platform next to mine and copied my position on the squares. "Why do I feel like I'm going to regret this?"

"Hey, have you got anything better to do?"

He considered me for a long moment, the vibe between us turning suddenly serious for reasons I didn't totally understand. "No," he said, the smirk coming back. "You want to dance? We'll dance."

The game kicked off with simple steps we both followed without any trouble. I could already feel that my rhythm was a little rusty after the years away from the game. As I got into the flow, Malcolm appeared to as well, his eyes narrowing with concentration. He was fast on his feet, I'd give him that. I found myself wondering if he did much actual dancing. What it might be like to face off with him on a club floor.

As the game sped up, I couldn't watch him anymore. All my attention had to stay on the screen and my feet. I stomped out a combo, grinning as I nailed it—and a current of magic tingled over my shoulders.

I caught myself before my head jerked around. Of course it was Malcolm. It wasn't even a new trick. He sounded like he was still keeping pace, but obviously he was aiming to get an advantage by distracting me. Well, we'd already seen that two could play at *that* game.

I worked through another combo and murmured a casting word with my breath. My hand swiveled in the air in time with my next few steps. A magical touch should have brushed down Malcolm's back.

His conjured current shifted a second later, dipping over my shoulder to lick my collarbone. My heartbeat thumped faster than I could blame on the exertion of the dancing. I teased my magic across his abdomen. He retaliated by sending his farther down to ripple across my breasts.

Heat flared all through my chest. I barely managed to complete the next few steps. With a twitch of my fingers, I sent my magic rushing down past the waist of his pants.

Malcolm's feet stumbled. He fell out of the pattern completely. Rather than try to recover, he spun around and grasped my arm—carefully, but abruptly enough to throw me off too.

I turned to face him, wrinkling my nose in annoyance and doing my best to hide the physical desire our game within the game had stirred up. Malcolm set his hand on my other arm, but he held himself apart from me, a foot between us, his dark brown eyes gleaming and his divinely handsome face lightly flushed.

"I think this game would be better played somewhere more private," he said. "Come up to my room?"

I couldn't lie—some part of me screamed *Yes!* at his invitation. But a larger part of me knew the second we stepped out of the arcade, all the past I'd been able to set aside would descend on me again… and I wasn't sure I was ready to throw caution to the wind.

"If you're not up to the challenge, you can just say so," I replied. "Lots of other games you can try your hand at here."

He stroked his thumbs over my arms. "Rory…"

The longing in his voice sobered me up. I looked him straight in the eyes. "I don't think that's a good idea. Not yet. I'm still… working through everything."

I thought he might leave after that admission. His hands dropped back to his sides. But he offered me a small smile and shrugged. "If you change your mind later, it's room 1506. You're welcome to drop by any time. Now, which of these relics are you going to try to kick my ass at next?"

Gratitude that he hadn't pushed the invitation, that he was willing to keep goofing around by my rules, brought a lump into my throat. I cocked my head as I considered our remaining options, but before I could pick, my phone chimed.

Lillian. As I read her message, even though I'd been expecting it, my spirits sank. I glanced up at Malcolm.

"Game time's over. I've got to go help them figure out exactly where my mother is."

Exactly where they were going to direct their brutal assault.

CHAPTER SEVENTEEN

Jude

It really was irritating how once you noticed something, you could never completely ignore it again, even if you'd managed to be oblivious to it for ages beforehand.

I had no idea how long my father had been ordering a few of his employees to keep an eye on me. Maybe it had been going on for years. Maybe it'd started the moment I'd moved out. Maybe the man I'd spotted by Killbrook Hall a few days ago had been the first intruder on his initial shift.

There was no way for me to tell. All I knew was that now that I'd picked up on my stalkers and their illusionary tricks, I couldn't make myself unaware, as much as I might have wanted to pretend they didn't exist.

I searched my bedroom and then the common room

when I had it to myself to make sure no spells or more mundane technology had been planted there, but my sphere of privacy ended beyond those walls. One or another figure was lurking around the green every time I left my dorm. Now and then I passed one in the halls. Someone slunk after me and my Physicality seminar classmates when we went out to the Casting Grounds to work on conjuring and transforming larger objects than the classroom would allow.

Their presence might not have annoyed me quite so much if I didn't have to wonder whether more people like that were spying on Rory now that she'd taken off for California. As if she didn't have enough to worry about while she tried to save her mother from the fucking joymancers without our own people recording her every move.

After the Physicality session, my stalker wavered between the trees some ten feet behind me, visible in a shaky blur at the edge of my vision when I turned to make a remark to one of my classmates. Frustration coiled in my gut.

This was ridiculous. I'd moved out so I could get *away* from my family. My supposed father hadn't wanted me anyway. Now I was faced with reminders of him and how little faith he had in me everywhere I looked. How was a guy supposed to concentrate on his studies? I'd like to make use of what actual talents I had.

Rather than heading back to the dorm or the scion lounge before my next class, I meandered past the Stormhurst Building toward the lake. My stalker let the distance between us extend on the open ground, but as soon as I veered off onto the path that led through the forest near the shore, he drew closer again. I waited until I'd walked about a quarter of a mile deep into the woods, and then I spun around and marched up to him in a few swift strides.

"Snap out of the illusion," I said, jabbing my finger in the general direction of where I thought the man's chest was. I aimed well enough to graze the fabric of his shirt.

The disguised form shifted as if to flee, but I had a good enough sense of his presence now to grab his arm before he could run. "Forget about that. I know you're here. I have to assume you know who *I* am. Do you really want to mess with a scion's magic?"

I hated leaning on that false label—and the false skills presumed to go with it—but the lie did serve me well. This guy had no idea I wasn't really who I was supposed to be. Dad would never have let *that* secret out.

After a moment's hesitation, my stalker waved the illusion away. I found myself staring at a skinny middle-aged man with a jutting chin and a suit that looked a little too tight. Then I registered the position of his free hand. He'd jerked it to the hilt of some sort of dagger shoved into his pocket.

I gave him an incredulous look. "What, were you planning on stabbing me? Do you have any idea the shitload of trouble you'd be in then?"

The man just stared back at me without flinching. "I don't answer to you."

The person he answered to was okay with him cutting

me open if he felt he needed to, then? My skin went suddenly cold. Had he been planning on doing that no matter what *I* did, just waiting for an ideal moment? Was Baron Killbrook so paranoid he'd risk offing me before his new heir had even arrived?

"Who *do* you answer to?" I asked, narrowing my eyes in what I intended to be a threatening expression. I drew a casting word into the back of my throat in case I had to fight for my life right now.

The guy didn't even bother to answer the question. He just glared at me obstinately. I released his arm to grasp the front of his shirt, letting an edge creep into my voice. "That's okay. I can figure it out. Why don't you go tell my father that your skills weren't up to the task. And that he'd have a whole lot less to worry about if he'd leave me alone."

I pushed the man away with a little shove. He scowled at me before swiveling on his heel and hurrying away. I scanned the forest quickly in case I had two stalkers on my trail today instead of just one. Nothing caught my eye.

Even without spotting another watcher, my pulse kept up a skittering beat as I headed back toward the main campus. Whatever he was thinking, Baron Killbrook wasn't playing around. I'd thought putting myself out of his way and out of his sight might be enough to keep things peaceful between us at least until my half-sister arrived. That clearly wasn't the case.

So, was I going to keep living like this, with him peering over my shoulder in every way he could and

possibly setting me up to be murdered at any moment...
or was I going to buck up and look the problem in the
face?

I stewed on that question as I walked. By the time I
reached my dorm, I couldn't stand the thought of sitting
back and waiting to see how he'd come at me next. I might
not be a Killbrook, but I had at least as much spine as a
scion should.

There was no point in calling Dad since he wouldn't
answer when he saw my number. I was pretty sure he'd
read a text, though.

*We have things to discuss. Let's do it without
intermediaries and without knives? You pick a place and I'll
meet you there.*

My heart thudded even harder as I hit send. I watched
my phone's screen for a few minutes before I accepted that
if he was going to answer, it wasn't going to be right away.
His lackey might not even have reported back to him yet.

Thankfully, my other class of the day was in
economics, which I'd always found relatively easy to pick
up simply because the Nary approach to finances could be
ridiculously complicated to the point of hilarity. I cruised
through the discussion on autopilot, tossing in a few wry
remarks as needed, and accepted the return of an essay on
which I'd gotten top marks. Well, perhaps if I couldn't
make a go of some kind of independent career in illusions,
I could set myself up at a non-magical university as a
professor of financial systems.

My phone's alert went off as I was heading out of class.

All my innards balled into a knot when I saw it was a message from my father.

He'd sent an address. No remark on my suggestion, no indication of how he felt about the meeting, just a street name and number and the town. Not exactly the warmest start to the conversation, but then, what had I expected? It was close to a miracle he'd agreed at all.

I didn't know what time he meant for me to be there, so I went straight to the garage. He could estimate how long it'd take me to make the trip from campus. He probably wanted me to jump at his command. Just this once, I'd indulge him.

As I drove across the countryside and on into the town he'd indicated, a deeper apprehension prickled through me.

My father might not want to talk at all. He might be using this as an excuse for an ambush. Bring me out to some isolated spot...

But the address he'd given me proved to be a trim four-story office building in the center of town. I parked on the street outside and walked up to the front door warily. A woman with thick framed glasses and dark lipstick met me at the entrance.

"Mr. Killbrook?" she said, all professional cool. "Please come with me."

This must be one of the fearmancer business holdings in the area. The baron families and other members of the community bought up commercial real estate here and there across the northeast so we'd have a base of operations nearby no matter what we were planning next. Quite likely Dad owned this one himself, if he was confident enough in whatever magical protections it held to want to have a potentially explosive conversation here.

The woman led me to an elevator, and we took it to the fourth floor. As she guided me to a door toward the end of the hall, my nose wrinkled. A faintly sickly smell hung in the air, as if the carpet had been recently deep-cleaned with some kind of god-awful cleaning fluid. A nice way to set the mood for this talk.

The woman opened the door and motioned me in. She closed it behind me, leaving me in a large, spartan office space that held only a couple of bookcases and a glass desk at the far end near the window. My supposed father sat behind the desk, his expression tight. His narrow face looked even more sallow than usual, not much different in shade from his pale hair.

"Here you are," he said flatly.

Here I was. I didn't see anywhere obvious to sit, so I settled for sauntering up to the desk and stopping a couple of feet away. "We can talk about anything here?" I asked.

"Whatever you have to say, go ahead and get on with it."

I wouldn't let his disdain rankle me the way it had so many times in the past. Rory was right. *I* hadn't done anything wrong. Everything this man hated about me was his own damned fault.

"I'd appreciate it if you'd call off your surveillance crew," I said. "I'm sure they'll have told you I'm not doing anything all that controversial. If you *want* to know what

I'm doing, you could just ask me, as difficult as that apparently is for you."

Baron Killbrook's gaze didn't waver. "I'll run my affairs as seems best to me. I didn't ask for your input."

I barely restrained a snort. "I didn't ask to be followed all over the place. I don't *belong* to you. And keep in mind that it's hardly going to look good to the other families if I make some kind of scene and it becomes obvious to all of them that you don't trust yourself to keep your heir in check without constant monitoring. I did you a favor making the confrontation private this morning. Next time I might be feeling less generous."

His lips tensed even more than they'd been before. "Is that a threat, Jude?"

He remembered my name. That was almost shocking in itself, considering how seldom he used it. I suppressed all the acidic comments I'd have liked to make in response.

"I don't see it that way," I said. "As far as I'm concerned, it's simply self-defense. You wouldn't have wanted to raise a scion who can't look after himself, would you?"

"I want a scion who won't ruin the family in the many other possible ways available to you."

I looked back at him, and suddenly all I felt was exhausted. What was the point of all this beating around the bush? I knew why he was afraid. He suspected I might know, and he was going to act as if I did to protect himself. I'd meant to save full honesty for when matters of his real heir were more settled, but fuck, why not get it over with and put an end to any need to worry about the man in front of me again?

"I hope you get one, then," I said. "We both know it's not me. I'm no more keen to see myself step up to the barony and be exposed as a fraud than you are."

Any remaining color drained from the man's face. "Jude—"

I barreled on. "I'm not asking you for anything. I'm not threatening you with anything. I just want to be done. I'll remove myself from your life the way I was already attempting to, and when my sister arrives I'll sign whatever documents you want transferring my supposed inheritance over to her—all of it, including the barony. We can leave it behind and never have to see or speak to or even think about each other again."

My father's expression twitched. He might have suspected I knew, but he probably hadn't expected I'd lay it out so baldly. He drew himself up straighter with a bristly air. "Whatever you think you're insinuating—"

I had to roll my eyes as I cut him off a second time. As if we really needed to keep up the pretense. "I'm not insinuating anything. I'm just saying you don't have anything to worry about from me when it comes to… anything about how I came into the family. I'm removing myself from it. That's what you want, isn't it? So let me do it."

His mouth opened and closed like a fish out of water. Then he stood up. "You don't get to give the orders around here."

Oh, for fuck's sake. "Fine," I said. "Whatever. Handle

it how you want. I was just trying to take something off your plate. Send me your forms for me to sign whenever you're ready. From here on, it's your problem, not mine."

I stalked out of the room without waiting for another blustering response, my pulse thumping raggedly but my spirits strangely light.

CHAPTER EIGHTEEN

Rory

The environment for the final locating spell couldn't have felt much more different from the overgrown field where we'd conducted the first two. Lillian, Maggie, and a few of their colleagues were staying in what must have been the hotel's largest executive suite, which was at least three times the size of my own large room. When one of the blacksuits let me in, I found they'd cleared the furniture from the main space, leaving a big oak dining table pressed to one wall, a sofa to another, with only glossy hardwood in the middle.

Conducting pieces scattered the floor, I assume to represent major landmarks in the city. The last few stones the blacksuits were setting down rapped against the polished boards. Lillian swept from one end of the room to the other in between her underlings, comparing them to a map she'd brought up on her phone. She adjusted the position of a piece here and another there before giving the space a satisfied nod.

I stopped at the edge of the room and considered the layout cautiously. "How closely are we going to be able to narrow down her location now that we're in the same city?"

"If all goes well, I expect we're likely to determine the exact building," Lillian said with a confident air. "Even if we're limited to a slightly larger area like a block, we should be able to determine the specific structure she's in with some in-person investigation. There'll be magic on the building—that much we can be sure of."

A lot of magic, wherever the joymancers were holding the most powerful of the fearmancer barons. If my mother had much power left in her now. I exhaled with a jitter of my nerves. "Okay. Should I stand in the middle like before?"

"Right here." She indicated a spot over a large casting stone. I walked over and planted my feet on either side of it. Lillian stepped back, and the other blacksuits joined her in forming a ring around the room. No one bothered with any special cleansing of me this time. I guessed that wasn't necessary with so much less distance to cover.

There were fifteen blacksuits altogether—a much larger force than had come to extract me from the joymancers' clutches. Lillian wasn't leaving anything to chance. I could only imagine how much destruction a group this large was capable of.

"Begin," Lillian said.

I closed my eyes as the murmurs rose, bracing myself.

This time, the magic crept up over me rather than hitting me in a deluge. The threads of it condensed and grew, sweeping through my body and out the top of my head in a now-familiar stream. The energy spread out more slowly this time too, only needing to stretch over this one city rather than the entire country. I could still breathe, still hear the voices intoning a casting word here and there, even as much of my awareness drifted off with the searching energy.

My birth mother was here. Somewhere in this city; maybe somewhere very close. I thought of the pictures and videos I'd seen of her from decades ago, of her smile as she'd cradled my infant self, of the bits and pieces Declan had been able to tell me about her associations with the other barons.

I didn't know what she'd be like now or even what she'd been like before, but I wanted to find out. The joymancers had stolen her from me and me from the life I'd been supposed to have, and while I didn't regret the time I'd had with Mom and Dad... It was time to set things right.

I had the vague impression of skimming over buildings and across busy streets. The magic tugged my senses one way and then another. Always the thrum of a sort of call rang through the energy, seeking out my mother's presence.

It should be even stronger here. That jolt of familiarity and anger...

I caught just a flicker of it, off to the right. My mind

itched to shoot straight toward it, but I caught myself and held it back.

If I could approach her location tentatively, before the blacksuits noticed—figure out some details they wouldn't grasp in time—maybe I could still keep some control over this situation. If I held the key to finding her, if they needed me for the final directions, they'd have to listen to me before they charged in.

That was my plan in theory, anyway. I edged my awareness toward that hint of my mother's presence, and two seconds later the magic flowing through me barreled past me, hurtling toward it.

That time, the sudden shift knocked the breath out of me. I had to struggle just to stay aware of the sensations around me rather than getting completely lost in the surge. My impression of her expanded, with a tug that ran right down to my heart. Even though I'd only called one woman this name in my entire life, I couldn't stop the thought from popping into my head.

Mom.

For a second, I could practically see her, just a few glints of silver in her dark brown hair, her indigo eyes wide and wild. Then the energy that'd been racing through me collapsed like a door slamming shut.

I stumbled but managed to stay on my feet this time. Lillian had been right about the local ceremony being less draining.

"What's the reading on that?" Lillian was saying, while a few of the other blacksuits bent over one of the conducting pieces. They muttered to each other or maybe to themselves in some casting. Then one straightened up.

"We've got an intersection in the radius—I'd say it's almost definitely one of the buildings on the corners."

Lillian snapped her fingers, striding through the room without regard for the other carved stones marking the floor, all business-like ferocity. "All right. You five head out there now and confirm the exact building. Scope out the defenses, magical and otherwise. I want a thorough report, every tiny enchantment covered." She spun on her heel. "You three, take an inventory on the other joymancer establishments we suspect in the city. Let's get an idea of how much backup this place can call on." She swiveled again, in the other direction. "The rest of you haven't used conductive weapons in a major offensive outside of training. Let's get you warmed up."

The first two groups she'd indicated dashed off in an instant. My stomach twisted as I watched them go. This was all happening so fast—and her last comments had chilled me. A major offensive was exactly what I'd hoped I could head off.

"Conductive weapons?" I repeated. I hadn't heard anyone talk about those before.

Maggie carried a thick canvas bag over from the other end of the suite. "This is stuff they don't teach at Blood U," she said, her usual smile bordering on a smirk. "No one's allowed to be in possession of one outside of official blacksuit business."

Lillian took the bag from her and drew out a long, knobby rod of carved stone, like a wizard's wand gone cancerous. The pocks on the knobby lumps told me at least some were hollowed out, made to store—and to amplify—spells the same way the stones littering the floor around us did. My pulse stuttered even without further explanation.

"We don't resort to using these often," Lillian said, giving the weapon a fond stroke. "They can give you the power to blaze through a whole line of defenses, but you do sacrifice some control. In this case, we can't afford to give those miscreants the chance to raise a larger defense. In and out as quickly as possible, and we'll get your mother back to you."

The eager gleam in her eyes made me even more unsettled. "But maybe they won't be necessary," I suggested carefully. "Once your people have scouted out the building, it might turn out that the joymancers have gotten a little lax with security over the years."

"I doubt it. We'll go in prepared, in any case." She glanced at me, still holding the weapon, and a thin smile crossed her face. "Do you want to try it?"

The question felt like a test I hadn't been prepared for. The thought of touching that thing, let alone sending any magic through it, made me queasy.

I raised my hands with an attempt at a self-deprecating smile. "Considering I have no training with those things at all, I'm not sure that's a good idea."

Maggie chuckled. "Aw, come on. I'm surprised you don't want to give the thing that could save your mother a spin."

What was she insinuating now? I hesitated, and Lillian hefted the bulbous rod. "I'll show you, then."

She aimed one end of the rod at the dining table. With a harshly whispered word, the weapon quivered. A wave of energy like a blast of wind shot from it and crashed into the table, smashing all four legs in the blink of an eye.

My jaw slackened. Lillian dropped the weapon back to her side. "That spell without the conductive powers would have simply dented the wood. That's the kind of power we can bring to bear."

"Do the joymancers have anything similar?" I asked as that additional horrible thought occurred to me.

"If they do, we'll just have to make sure to hit them first and harder." She patted my arm and tucked the weapon back into its bag. "You don't need to worry about us. We know what we're doing. And you'll stay safely here at the hotel while this is going down."

I caught hold of the only other excuse to protest that I could think of like a lifeline. "I can't help worrying," I said. "You're the closest thing to family I've had since I was rescued, and my mom will be part of the fighting too. Are you sure there's no way we could negotiate her release now that we know she's there?"

Lillian snorted. "The joymancers would just be that much more prepared to push back. Besides, they deserve to pay for what they did to her. I'm looking forward to seeing plenty of their blood spilled."

Her voice and her expression had gone so hard I couldn't

think of anything I could say that might sway her—and that wouldn't start making her suspicious of me. I wavered there for a moment with nausea percolating through my belly.

"How soon do you think you'll be able to move on the building?"

She rubbed her jaw. "I'd imagine we should be able to gather the information quickly enough to plan an assault for tomorrow night. You won't have to wait much longer."

And I didn't have much more time to figure out some kind of alternate plan. I forced a smile.

"I know you'll bring her back," I said, and fled the suite so I could figure out how *I* could make that happen without bodies littering the streets.

CHAPTER NINETEEN

Rory

Halfway down the hall to my hotel room, a wave of dizziness washed over me. I stopped to catch my balance against the wall. A pang shot through my gut, and it occurred to me that while it was only late afternoon here in California, by my body's adapted northeastern schedule, it was well past when I'd normally have eaten dinner. Intense spells on an empty stomach wasn't a great combination, especially if I wanted to come up with some brilliant plan.

I detoured the elevator and grabbed a croissant sandwich and a fruit salad in the café at the front of the lobby. My familiar would be happy to share those. My gaze darted over the lobby as I hurried back to the elevator, watching for Malcolm or the blacksuits, as if they'd be able to tell just by looking at me that I wasn't feeling totally onboard with the plans in the works.

I made it to my room unhindered, but the restlessness I'd managed to briefly chase away in the arcade had gripped me again, ten times as insistently. While Deborah hopped onto the desk to nibble at the grapes and piece of sandwich I broke off for her, I stayed on my feet. Each bite of my hasty dinner stuck in my throat before going down. In the back of my mind, the memory of my parents' deaths kept replaying—gurgles of breath, blood splashed on white tiles.

Some joymancers had done awful things—but so had some fearmancers. *Neither* group deserved to be slaughtered for it. But how the hell could I possibly convince Lillian to try another way? She didn't just see a full-out massacre as the best option; she relished the idea.

Has something gone wrong? Deborah asked, looking up from her meal at my fifth pacing of the room.

"We did the final locating ceremony," I said. "They pretty much know where the joymancers have my mother now. And they're planning on ripping their way through anyone who stands between them and her."

Maybe even Naries, like I'd worried about before. No matter how late at night the blacksuits launched their attack, there could be passersby, or the effects of the magic might extend beyond the one building. Lillian had admitted the conducting weapons allowed less accuracy. And I knew as well as anyone that most fearmancers didn't give a shit about the lives of people without magic.

Guilt wrapped tight around my chest. "I'm the only one who knows what's going to happen and who cares enough to want to change it. But I don't have any idea how. I tried talking to Lillian, but she's too caught up in her revenge." I dropped down onto the edge of my bed with a rough exhalation. "I'm supposed to be the most powerful mage the university has seen in years. What good is that if I can't do anything to stop dozens of people from dying?"

You're up against an entire society that believes in brutality, Deborah said, scurrying across the table to me. *It'd be hard for anyone to push back. You should feel proud of how well you've held your own so far. You're a credit to your parents.*

She meant my joymancer parents, of course. And yeah, I had to think that Mom and Dad would have said the same thing. They'd encouraged me to speak up for what I believed in, but they'd also believed in being aware of your limits.

That didn't help me save any lives, though.

"It's my fault," I said quietly. "If I hadn't helped them with their spells…"

Do you really think they'd have let you bow out? That woman stole a little piece of you to help her already. And… I understand that this is your family, Rory. I don't blame you for wanting to free your birth mother, even if I can't imagine she'll be the mother you deserve. But perhaps she has changed in the time the Conclave has kept her in custody. I'm not sure them holding onto her is worth the risk of bloodshed.

Her words brought a spark of hope into my chest, tenuous but bright.

If my adoptive parents had believed the things they did, if Deborah could accept me despite my heritage, there had to be other joymancers who didn't see the different types of magic in black and white. Who'd recognize my good intentions—who'd realize that a compromise would be better for both sides.

I could be careful. I had plenty of magic to defend myself. And if they didn't listen, at least I might learn something that would help mitigate the damage.

Pros and cons, Dad would have said. *Go!*

Pros: I might be able to negotiate my birth mother's release without anyone even getting hurt. If not, I'd at least get a closer look at the Conclave's inner workings. And I'd be doing *something* other than sitting back and letting the carnage happen.

Cons: The Conclave might see me as an enemy and try to hurt *me*. If I wasn't careful, I could reveal too much and ruin any chance of getting my mother back.

I sucked my lower lip under my teeth. Those were big risks. But I'd have Deborah with me, and she could vouch for me in her own way. I'd convinced the other scions, even Malcolm, that not every joymancer was necessarily horrible—surely I could convince the joymancers that I wasn't horrible either when I was right there in front of them. If I had to go through a little pain along the way before they listened… wouldn't the outcome be worth it?

I was in a special position, really, as a fearmancer raised by joymancers. I was a bridge between the two sides. This might be my only chance in who knew how long to really make use of that fact. How could I not try?

The sun was still shining brightly beyond my window. As long as I was back before tomorrow morning, I suspected the blacksuits would be too busy making plans to check on me.

"Deborah," I said. "You mentioned the Conclave's headquarters aren't far from here?"

They're just east of San Francisco, in the Berkeley area, my familiar said, perking up. *It would be an expensive ride, but I'd imagine you'd find someone willing to take you that far.*

Money wasn't a problem. I sat up straighter and reached for my suitcase. "Let's see if I can prevent a total disaster, then."

My luggage didn't contain many clothing options, but I had a casual pair of slacks and a T-shirt that felt more appropriate for a mission where I might need to do a little running. I changed quickly and held out my arm so Deborah could leap onto my hand.

I ran into my first hitch when I returned to the lobby. A couple of blacksuits were standing near the front doors. They wouldn't think anything of me wandering around inside the hotel, but I didn't want them wondering why I'd left or where I was going.

I'd studied for the possibility of needing to stay out of view, though. I ducked into the arcade room, which was empty again, and concentrated on my whole body as I murmured, "Mirror."

The illusionary effect spread over my limbs and torso as I willed the magic from the base of my throat. I said the casting word again, feeling the energy tingle up over my face. When I stepped in front of one of the games, the glass screen reflected only the room around me.

Perfect. With a skip of my pulse, I headed out into the lobby.

I gave the blacksuits a wide berth, pausing just for a second in hearing range in case their conversation held any interest. They were discussing the possibility of calling more blacksuits down from New York. More bodies in the fray—exactly what we needed. I slipped out the door feeling even more of a sense of urgency than before.

I walked several blocks until I felt sure no one who'd recognize me was likely to stumble on me and then ordered an Uber on my phone. Deborah waited with me, her tiny claws hooked into the collar of my shirt beneath my hair. It took a few minutes to locate a driver who'd make the trip out to the address she'd given me, but then I was on my way.

There should be at least a few people on hand at the headquarters no matter the time, my familiar said as the car zoomed toward the freeway. *I don't know how much they'll necessarily know about you. Your best bet for a starting point is giving them my name: Deborah Penfound. They'll be able to look me up in their files and see that I was assigned to you. Any questions they have about how you've conducted yourself, they can confirm through my memories and impressions.*

I nodded, not able to answer her directly without the driver thinking I was crazy. My lungs tightened as we left the hotel and my new associates farther and farther behind.

My parents had believed in the Conclave, I reminded myself. And while the joymancers might have been afraid of me, they *had* let Mom and Dad continue to raise me even after I'd reached the age when I might have developed my magic despite their suppressive spells. If I didn't treat them like an enemy, I wouldn't give them any reason to treat me like one either.

We'd been on the road for almost an hour when my phone chimed. I'd left my purse back at the hotel but had tucked the phone into the pocket of my pants.

Malcolm had texted me. *Ceremony over? We could grab dinner—and then I'd like to challenge you to a Street Fighter rematch.*

My mouth twitched with a faint smile, but I wasn't going to tell him what I was really up to. He'd never have approved of this mission. I remembered his enraged reaction to the news that the joymancers had imprisoned my mother way too clearly. Chances were if he found out what I was doing, he'd call on Lillian to haul me back.

Sorry, already ate and ceremony + jetlag took a lot out of me, I wrote back. *Going to crash early. But you're on for that rematch in the morning.*

Hopefully that would satisfy him for the time being. I didn't think he'd come knocking on my hotel room door after how careful he'd been about my boundaries since the boathouse incident this summer, but better not to leave him hanging too much.

After we got off the freeway, the driver wound through a residential neighborhood with neat lawns and lots of trees shading the streets. He stopped in front of a large building in pale yellow stucco that took up almost half of the block it was on. I gathered my nerve, thanked him for the drive, and got out.

A faint floral scent drifted to me from farther down the road. A few kids were playing street hockey the next block over, their shouts and laughter adding to the sunny atmosphere. It was hard to believe people who'd place their base of operations in a place like this could be all that malicious.

I still had to be careful, though. I touched my phone in my pocket, glanced around, and took it out so I could tuck it out of sight under one of the shrubs along the front edge of the lawn. Better not to give the joymancers direct access to all my contacts. Then I reached to my neck so I could scoop up Deborah and walked to the broad front door with her cupped in my hands in front of me like an offering.

The building had no sign on the lawn or over the door to indicate it was anything other than a house, if a very large one. I guessed the joymancers had no reason to advertise that fact to anyone who didn't already know who they were. A tingle of magical energy brushed over my feet on my way up the front walk, but I couldn't tell what effect it had. If it was some sort of security spell, it didn't stop me.

I rang the doorbell and waited for several anxious seconds. Then a calm female voice crackled through the intercom mounted beside the door frame.

"What's your business here?"

I leaned close to the speaker so I didn't have to raise my voice. "I'd like to speak with someone from the Conclave. I'm here with Deborah Penfound, who can vouch for me—she suggested I come. My parents were

Rafael and Lisa Franco, and they always spoke highly of the Conclave."

I hoped throwing in that last bit would go farther toward showing I wasn't fully allied with the fearmancers.

"Hold on a moment," the voice said, and the intercom went silent. I resisted the restless urge to shift on my feet.

This is all standard procedure, Deborah reassured me. *I can't imagine they'll take more than a minute or two. They might want to check the area to make sure you haven't brought anyone else with you, but then they'll have no reason to distrust you.*

The door swung open just as she finished speaking. A man who looked around thirty, with rectangular glasses perched on his hooked nose, peered out at me. His gaze slid to the mouse in my hands.

I held her up. "This is Deborah. And I'm—I was Rory Franco. If you have any questions about my intentions or where I've been, she's told me she's happy to show you whatever she can through insight spells."

I felt a little ridiculous talking about what to the man in front of me must have looked like a regular mouse, but to my relief he nodded. "Why don't you come in?" he said. "I think we'll have a lot to discuss."

That sounded promising. I inhaled deeply as I stepped over the threshold, the scent of freshly baked bread tickling down my throat from somewhere deeper in the building. The walls were painted a warm cream, and the rhythmic sound of typing filtered from a nearby room.

The man motioned me down the hall, shutting the door behind me.

"I'm sorry to drop in without any warning," I started. "I didn't have a lot of choice. I—"

Three figures hurtled through the inner doorway I'd just come up on. Casting words tripped over their lips before I could summon any sort of defense in my surprise.

A spell slammed into my knees, locking them together and knocking me to the floor. Another slapped over my mouth, silencing the cry that tried to escape my lips. My shoulder jarred against the floor. Deborah tumbled from my hands.

A woman with sharp green eyes leaned over and snapped the necklace with my dragon charm from my neck. "There's magic on this," she told the guy next to her. "Test its capabilities."

I strained to speak against the spell, but it bound me too tightly. Panic flared through my chest. Where had Deborah gone?

The woman's expression hardened even more as she straightened up, staring down at me. "We can't be too careful. This girl murdered her own parents."

Then, with a jerk of her hand, my mind went black.

CHAPTER TWENTY

Connar

Like me, my familiar didn't have to do anything other than exist to generate a certain amount of fear. People saw the python cruising through the field or looping across my shoulders and gave off the same tickle of anxiety they did when they saw me striding toward them, strong, solid, and with a murderous family reputation.

I wasn't sure Rex minded or cared—he wasn't the most emotive familiar, although I could sense his satisfaction as he got to stretch his muscles winding through the grass— and frankly, most of the time it worked in our favor. We didn't get hassled. I got a steady supply of fear to fuel my magic. But every now and then I couldn't help thinking it wasn't completely fair to either of us.

A couple of juniors crossing the field startled at the shifting of the grass. They veered to the side to put more distance between us and them. They'd have to get used to a lot worse than snakes if they were going to survive Blood U—or the rest of fearmancer society, for that matter. Shaking my head, I straightened up and snapped my fingers. "Rex. Here."

The python slithered over and twined up my arm when I reached for him. He settled into his favorite position: lounging across my shoulders.

On my way back to Ashgrave Hall, I ran into Declan on the green. He tipped his head in greeting, looking like he was on his way to someplace or another he needed to be soon, but the sight of him jostled loose an urge I couldn't suppress. I held out my hand to stop him.

"Have you heard anything from Rory?" I asked.

He gave me a smile that was both knowing and sympathetic. "Not so far. She won't have even been in California that long yet. I'm sure when she has news, she'll share it with all of us."

I couldn't picture her favoring any of us over another either, but somehow asking made the worrying a little easier. At least Malcolm was out there with her. There was a hell of a lot I could have criticized about how he'd treated the Bloodstone scion in her first few months here, but now that he'd come around, I knew how quick he'd be to fight for her if he needed to. I only wished I could have been out there too.

"I know," I said. "It's just hard not to wonder what's going on out there."

"Tell me about it." He paused. "Were you expecting a visit from your mother?"

My back stiffened. "No. Why?"

"I saw her getting out of her car over at the parking lot. Maybe she just has business with one of the staff. But I figured you wouldn't mind a heads up if it's more than that."

"Thanks," I said, and he set off again. My jaw tightened as I turned toward the dorm building. What the hell did my mother want now?

A few of my dormmates were hanging out in the common room. They nodded to me, but I caught the flashes of wariness. One of them badly hid a grimace at the sight of Rex. I was too occupied with what Declan had told me to summon much offense.

I opened the door to my bedroom cautiously, but my mother hadn't made another surprise visit here. I guessed she wouldn't have wanted to march right in with so many other students around this early in the evening. She hadn't contacted me in any other way, though. If she'd come for a chat, where was she?

I lowered Rex into his terrarium, and he curled up on his stone beneath the lights. He'd done a little hunting in the forest a few days ago, and with a python's eating habits, that meant he was good for at least another week.

Some of the other students enjoyed tormenting their familiars with a mix of harsh and kind treatment, getting extra spurts of fear and anxiety from that, but I'd always found that approach sickening. The familiar was supposed to be our partner in creating magic. I checked to make sure he had everything he needed and then left him to his nap.

With a few quick words, I set the magical security on my door back in place. Then I headed out of the building. I'd meant to get started on an essay on the theory of Physicality magic that Professor Viceport had assigned to the Physicality specialists, but I wasn't going to be able to concentrate knowing my mother might turn up at any moment.

Her car, a sleek BMW, was parked in the lot out front of Killbrook Hall like Declan had said. As I made for it, my mother herself emerged from the hall, loping down the stairs with her brisk athletic strides. She caught sight of me and raised an eyebrow in question.

"Were you looking for me?" she asked in her typical brusque way.

"I thought maybe you were looking for me," I said. But obviously she hadn't been. She'd only come to speak to one of the professors—or Ms. Grimsworth? What kind of business could she have had with them that she'd needed to carry out in person? Rory had mentioned that a few of the professors or their relatives were on the list of co-conspirators she'd gotten from her mentor.

Or maybe my mother *had* meant to come looking for me next, and she was simply enjoying putting me off-balance by pretending otherwise. She motioned to the car. "Since you're here, there is something we should discuss. But preferably more privately. Let's take a quick drive."

Well, I'd asked for this. And if she had something she wanted to talk about, it was probably better to get it over with.

I sank into the front passenger seat. The car had the

tang of the sharp citrusy stuff the Stormhurst staff used to maintain the leather.

My mother dropped into the driver's seat and had the engine growling within a second of shutting the door. With practiced efficiency, she jerked the wheel and brought us around to the road into town.

"Word seems to be spreading quickly, at least through the baron families," she said as we roared toward the woods. "I'd guess you already know about Baron Bloodstone's impending return."

She sounded completely confident that Rory's mother would be rescued and be well enough to take up the barony almost immediately. The sinews stood out in her wiry hands where she gripped the steering wheel, but the glint in her steely eyes was all happy anticipation.

"I do," I said. If I hadn't already known about it from Rory, Malcolm obviously would have told the rest of us. "That was unexpected."

"Unexpected, but very welcome. Her heir will be *her* responsibility, and we can get on with things the way we meant to without any further hassle."

She cocked her head at the road in front of us and pulled over to the shoulder with a lurch. The shadows of the trees stretched long across the car. We were far enough from both campus and the town that I couldn't see any sign of either, only the forest looming darkly on either side.

My mother muttered a few words that I assumed were a security casting of some sort—making sure no sound could leave the car, or maybe even disguising it from view so no one who happened to pass by would realize we were sitting here talking. Then she swiveled in her seat to face me.

"You've still been romantically entangled with the Bloodstone scion," she said. It wasn't a question, but then, how likely was that to have changed in the week since I'd stood up for Rory at her hearing?

The memory of telling Rory I loved her, of her saying it back—as exhilarating as soaring through the air with her holding onto my dragon form—quivered through my mind. I schooled my expression as impassive as I could. Those reactions wouldn't fit with the story I wanted my mother to believe.

"I have," I said. "After the hearing, she trusts me completely."

"Hmm. Well, at least we can get some satisfaction out of knowing she'll be heartbroken as a little payback for the trouble she's caused us. The moment she comes back from this mission to California, I want you to break things off with her. As callously as you know how."

I blinked at her, my stomach sinking. I'd thought we'd gotten past the idea of breaking Rory's heart—I'd managed to convince my parents once that staying with the Bloodstone scion worked in their favor as well as mine.

"There are still so many ways it could be useful for me to have her ear," I said, scrambling for any excuse I could find. Verbal sparring wasn't exactly one of my strengths. "Why throw away the work I've already put in?"

My mother shrugged. "We don't have to care what's going on with the little bitch anymore. Like I said, she'll be her mother's responsibility. And her mother will be making the calls for the Bloodstone barony."

"For now. Rory will be baron eventually."

"And in the meantime, she's making a mockery of her family name. I don't want to see the Stormhurst name dragged through any mud alongside her."

"I can look after myself," I said stiffly, but my mind was racing for some other argument to offer. I couldn't throw my relationship with Rory away. If I'd thought doing that would help her, I would have in an instant, but just to satisfy my mother? Hell, no.

The time I had with Rory was the most happiness I'd felt since I'd ruined Holden's life.

I latched onto one final effort. "Won't Baron Bloodstone be upset about a Stormhurst causing her daughter that much pain?"

My mother snorted. "Althea will be just as disturbed by her daughter's behavior—and just as eager to see her brought to heel—as we've been." Her eyes narrowed as she considered me. "For someone who was supposedly only using the girl, you seem awfully reluctant to break things off with her. I'm starting to think you've fallen for her."

The words sprang to my tongue to deny it, but at the same time an unexpected sense of resolve rose up inside me.

What was the point in denying it? I wasn't going to follow my mother's orders anyway, and she'd know that I hadn't. Didn't Rory deserve a guy who'd stand up for her not just in front of a judge but to his own parents? Who was willing to own his feelings for her even when it might make his life a little more difficult?

What could my mother do to me, really, that I couldn't handle? I was her only real heir. It was time I started acting like I knew that.

I looked back at my mother, letting the strength I could feel coiled through my body harden my gaze. "If I have, isn't that my business, not yours? I'm twenty years old. I think that's past the point when you should be dictating who I spend my time with."

A flash of surprise crossed my mother's face before she managed to contain it. I caught it with a spark of triumph that lasted until her mouth set in a grim line.

"You need to be brought to heel too, then. And that's my responsibility as both your mother and baron. We'll see what we can make of this… misguided infatuation."

"It isn't misguided and it's not an infatuation," I said.

She ignored me, gunning the engine again. My heart lurched, and my hand shot to the door. Alarm rang through me. I had to get out of here, away from her.

I yanked at the door handle, but it didn't budge. My mother chuckled and hit the gas. As the car sped onto the road, I spun toward her, just in time for her to whip a spell at me with a single snapped casting word.

My body slammed back into the seat. My jaw locked shut. My muscles strained, but I couldn't move any part of me as much as half an inch. All I could do was stare straight ahead as my mother tore off to some unknown destination.

CHAPTER TWENTY-ONE

Rory

I came to on a hard wooden chair in a room the size of a closet. Glancing up, my head still a little foggy, I realized it might very well *be* a closet, just an empty one. A rung ran across one side near the top of the space, and the open doorway in front of me appeared to lead out into a larger room rather than a hallway.

Cuffs made of thick metal encircled my wrists, weighing them down on my lap. Otherwise, I didn't seem to be restrained at all. I stood up, braced myself against a rush of dizziness, and took a tentative step toward the doorway.

It was a good thing my hands were locked in front of me. They, instead of my face, banged into an invisible but sharply solid barrier across the doorway. I jerked back as lances of pain shot up my forearms. My calves jarred against the chair behind me. There wasn't a whole lot of room to maneuver.

Which I guessed was the idea. A woman stepped into view—the woman with the penetrating green eyes who'd taken my necklace and accused me of murdering my parents. She eyed me warily, her square face framed by a chin-length bob of mixed gray and nut-brown.

"You're not going anywhere," she said. "Whatever plans you had for harming the Conclave, you can forget about them."

Okay. I'd known the first part of this confrontation might be hard. I forced myself to sit back down on the stool where I could rest my arms at a more comfortable angle.

"I didn't come so I could hurt the Conclave," I said. "Admitting who I am upfront and walking in here peacefully wouldn't have been the smartest approach if I had, would it?"

"That depends on how much access you were hoping to get before you revealed your true intentions."

I breathed in and out as calmly as I could, holding my temper. It made sense for her to be suspicious of me. She had no idea what had happened to me or where I'd been for the last six months.

"Why don't we start by clearing a few things up, then?" I said. "I had nothing to do with my parents' deaths. I didn't even know what was going on when the fearmancer squad came to get me. I tried to *save* Mom and Dad. But there wasn't a whole lot I could do considering I didn't even know I had magic, let alone have any training in how to use it."

The woman folded her arms over her chest. Her gaze flicked briefly to the side, making me suspect someone else was following this conversation out of my sight.

"If you were an unwilling victim, where have you been all this time? Why didn't you reach out to the Conclave for help?"

Seriously? "I didn't exactly have a chance. The only joymancers I knew were my parents, and they were gone. I couldn't have taken off across the country without the fearmancers chasing me down in an instant. It wasn't like I could look you all up in a phone directory or something."

"But you made it here now."

"Yes. I—" I hesitated, not sure it'd be wise to reveal my exact reasons for being here. There wasn't any point in bringing up my birth mother and tipping off the joymancers that we were aware they were keeping her captive until I was in a position to start negotiating instead of just defending myself. "I was able to take part in a trip out here. My familiar told me how to find this place. Deborah can confirm everything I've told you. If you've looked at the records, you must know she's more than just a mouse."

The woman let out a huff. "A human mind trapped in an animal—no doubt easily manipulated. I wouldn't trust anything we saw in that little rodent head at this point. Why bother looking at it?"

My heart sank. I shifted my wrists on my lap, the cuffs chaffing my skin. They must have been like the ones the blacksuits had put on me when I'd first been taken into custody for Imogen's murder—blocking my magical abilities. I couldn't sense a hint of the magic that'd been collected behind my sternum.

"You could look in my head at my memories, then," I offered, even though the thought of making myself vulnerable to this woman left my skin crawling. If taking that risk made my case for me, it'd be worth it.

But she was already shaking her head. "You'd have come prepared. I have no reason to believe anything you say—or anything you show me."

I groped for some other proof I could give her. "The necklace you took off me—that charm was one my parents gave me. I wouldn't be wearing something I got from joymancers if I didn't still care about them and miss them."

"Again," the woman said, "I have no reason to believe anything you say." She rocked back on her heels, her jaw working. "The Francos were always too easy on you. They believed the toxic stain wouldn't show through as long as you never had the opportunity to work your magic. And yet you fell in with our enemies so easily. With the people who killed them, if your story is true."

"I hate what the fearmancers did to Mom and Dad," I said quietly. "And they're not all like that. I've been trying to make a difference in the fearmancer community as much as I can. I don't know what you want from me, if you're not going to believe anything. What can I do or say that would count?" Or were they going to keep me locked up here until the end of time?

Where the hell was Deborah, anyway? I didn't see any sign of her in the room. Had she tried to approach them? Had they caught her and shut her away like they had me?

Or had she fled back to her own people the first chance she got? Maybe she'd never expected the Conclave to welcome me after all. She'd just wanted to come home, to get away from the constant threat of living among the fearmancers.

The thought brought a lump into my throat. I didn't want to believe that. I hadn't always agreed with Deborah's opinions, but I'd felt as if she'd cared about me, as if she'd wanted to help me.

The woman didn't look at all moved by my plea. "It isn't up to me to decide what happens to you," she said. "When everyone who needs to be part of that discussion is here, we'll make a decision."

I came here to help you! I wanted to shout at her. But I couldn't see how it would do me any good after what she'd already said.

She stepped to one side, and a man came into view— short but with a frame so ropey with muscle it gave him plenty of presence anyway. His glower made me tense on the chair before he even spoke.

"I want to know more about the trip that brought you here," he said in a voice that managed to sound like a threat without actually threatening me with anything. "How did you get here? How many other fearmancers are with you? Where are they staying? What is their purpose here? If you start answering questions and we can confirm they're correct, then maybe we'll believe you've defected."

My chest tightened. The problem was, I *hadn't* defected. I was trying to keep the interests of both sides in mind. As much as I was repulsed by Lillian's desire for violent revenge, I didn't want to see the joymancers slaughter the blacksuits like they had my father and Declan's mother either.

"I came to you because I don't want to see *anyone* hurt," I said. "I'm not going to point you in some direction so you can go attack those people. My parents, the joymancers who raised me, wouldn't have believed that was the right thing to do. That's how they raised me. So if you want to blame them for anything, blame them for teaching me *too* well, not for slacking off somehow."

The guy bristled. "You have no idea what you're talking about. Sometimes we have to act to defend ourselves. If 'your' people have come into our territory, then we have every right to carry out that defense."

I stared back at him, my irritation growing. "And what's it called when you go up into fearmancer territory and start attacking them there?"

"I'm not going to debate our strategies with you of all people," he snapped. "Is that your position? You're refusing to talk? It might get a lot more unpleasant for you later if you don't cooperate now."

Ah, there was the actual threat. I gritted my teeth. "I came here because I wanted to help you. If you're going to torture me as a thank you, then you're not exactly convincing me I chose the right side. That's up to you. But it sure doesn't make you look like the good guys in this scenario."

The guy muttered something inarticulate under his breath and marched away. I waited to see if he or the woman who'd questioned me first would return, but what I could see of the room in front of me remained still and silent.

They might not come back until they'd had their discussions. Until they were ready to torture me for answers... or until they'd decided to do something else with me. Lock me up like they presumably had my mother? Kill me? A chill crept over my skin.

I wanted to hope that someone they were waiting for would be more reasonable, but after the conversation I'd just had, that was seeming less and less likely. Fucking hell.

I had to figure out a way out of this. If I was still stuck here the next time the blacksuits came to talk to me at the hotel, if they realized I'd vanished... I might have created two bloodbaths instead of one. And after they'd blazed their way through the Conclave headquarters, I wasn't sure any fearmancer would trust me any more than the joymancers did. Not when I'd basically proven myself a traitor.

Without knowing how long I'd been knocked out for, I had no idea how much longer I even had to make my case—or my escape.

CHAPTER TWENTY-TWO

Rory

My butt was starting to go numb and my wrists were tingling from the pressure of the cuffs when a small white body slipped through the closet doorway. Whatever magical barrier the joymancers had put in place there, it apparently didn't apply to animals. Maybe it could sense that Deborah was a joymancer on whatever level she still was.

She scrambled up my pantleg and perched on my knee. Mice didn't have the most expressive faces, but her beady black eyes held an undeniable sadness. She nuzzled my hand just above the edge of the cuff.

I'm so sorry, she said in my head.

"It's not your fault they're being asshats," I muttered under my breath. At least, I couldn't see how it was. She wouldn't have come back to me like this if she'd been conspiring against me, would she?

Unless she'd come to try to convince me to give away the blacksuits' whole plan to the joymancers.

I encouraged you to come here. I told you they'd listen, that they'd believe you... She buried her face in her front paws. *I thought with your history, and with me here—but they won't even believe me. I tried to present myself, and that man who threatened you came after me like I was a pest to be exterminated. After hearing the way they talked to you, this was obviously a mistake. I don't understand... I know how much they distrust the fearmancers, but your situation is hardly the same...*

So much anguish came through in her voice that my heart squeezed. I had the urge to stroke her back in the way that would have comforted both of us a little, but it was too awkward with the cuffs in place. Instead I could only grimace.

"So, I guess you don't have any idea how we could convince them that I don't have some evil plan? Have you seen any of the mages who arranged for you to be my familiar? They must have trusted you when they picked you for the job."

I haven't yet. Maybe someone who was involved will be coming for their 'discussion.' But from the sounds of things, they see me as contaminated somehow by having been with you among the fearmancers. As if I'd be swayed that easily.

Her indignation brought a faint smile to my lips in spite of everything, but the twist of tension in my chest remained. I drew in a shaky breath. I had to be careful how much I said out loud. We couldn't know whether the joymancers might be monitoring us either directly or magically.

"I don't know if I can do anything good by staying here," I said. "It seems like anything else I say is only going to make things worse for everyone."

I might be able to help you get out of this place. We'll need to give them a little time to relax their guard and feel we're totally subdued before I'm likely to get away with what I'm thinking… But I'm not letting them treat you like some kind of criminal. My goodness, the fearmancers *were more accepting of your background than this bunch.*

"Yeah." And I'd promised myself I'd find *some* way to make the conflict tomorrow easier on both sides by coming here, even if it wasn't through negotiation. I couldn't say I'd learned much about the joymancers' operations so far.

"I'm going to stand up," I said. Deborah took the cue to scamper up my sleeve to my shoulder. I got to my feet, shaking the prickles from my legs, and eased closer to the doorway, careful of the barrier I now knew was there.

I couldn't see anything that looked useful to report on. The room appeared to be a sleeping area, with a couple of twin beds against the far wall and a matching dresser and vanity on either side of the doorway opposite them. All I could see of the hallway the entrance led to was a rectangle of brighter light and a pale section of wall. Super helpful.

How much would the joymancers have figured out already? They couldn't assume we'd come here because of my mother, right? After all, they'd had her for seventeen years without the fearmancers realizing, and I hadn't given away anything to suggest this "visit" had anything to do with her. I didn't think I'd screwed anything up yet, other than my own freedom.

But I didn't want to be yet another problem for Lillian and her blacksuits to solve. I'd look like a traitorous idiot. And even if Deborah and I could manage to escape, I'd still *feel* like an idiot if I couldn't find some way to do more than simply not create an additional disaster. These people might be treating me horribly, but that didn't mean I was eager to see dozens of mages like them dead tomorrow night.

Come on, Rory. *Think.*

The joymancers refused to believe I had anything but malicious intentions. If I tried to bargain with them, they'd only focus on the planned assault and assume my attempts to work out a deal that would leave both sides uninjured were a ploy rather than genuine. If they knew the fearmancers were here to break out my mother, they'd double the security, and more people would die on one side or the other. They might already have increased their efforts just in case, because of my presence.

If there was something I could say that would convince them to *reduce* the security so at least fewer joymancers would end up in the blacksuits' line of fire... Or to give us an opening that Lillian would have to use at a time when they'd need to be more cautious about how much magic they threw around in front of the Nary population...

A plan started to come together in my mind. I couldn't tell if it was a very good one, but I knew one thing for sure

—any mention of my mother or the building she was in would only put the joymancers more on guard and make the assault harder. Unless I could unsettle them so much that they brought her right out of the building for us.

Before I took this gamble, though, I needed to be sure that the joymancers were listening to what I said in here… without them realizing that I knew.

Deborah had tucked herself behind my hair again. I couldn't send words into her head the way she could with me, but the familiar connection did still go both ways. I should be able to convey feelings, impressions…

I focused on the small warmth of her body and the need welling inside me: for her to slip off of me and out into the hall as stealthily as possible, to keep watch, to spy, to see what she could see. My fingers curled toward my palms as I put all my concentration into projecting those images.

I couldn't tell how much might have passed on to her, but after several seconds, without a word, Deborah darted down my side and the back of my leg. She left the room hugging the wall closely. I waited until I was sure she'd be in a decent position in the hall. Then I wriggled my wrists.

"You know," I said quietly, as if she were still with me, "I think one of the cuffs might be a little loose. If I can work one hand out, maybe I can cast enough magic to get us out of here."

I twisted my hands against the cuffs in case the joymancers had some kind of visual on me too, counting down the seconds in my head. I wanted to give them enough time to react but not so much that one of them reached me and gave away their monitoring. The metal dug into my skin.

"Damn it," I said a little louder. "Nope, they're not going to budge."

I might have heard the faintest scuff of a footstep from the hall. Sinking back in my chair as if defeated, I kept my ears perked. But it wasn't my own senses I was counting on.

Deborah scurried back into the room a minute later and clambered up beside me. *If you were hoping to provoke some kind of response, it looked like you did,* she said. *I'm not sure what set them off, but shortly after I went into the hall, one of the joymancers came bursting out of a room farther down. She made it about halfway here before one of the others called her back. He said something about a "false alarm."*

Because I hadn't been on the verge of escape after all. I'd have smiled if I hadn't been afraid of giving away part of my plan.

This next part… this was the real gamble. I could be making an even bigger mess of things. I had to at least try, though. That was why I'd come to California in the first place.

The joymancers hadn't believed me about my good intentions… but they might very well believe me about malicious schemes, especially if I made a show of holding certain details back until I thought they couldn't hear me.

"I have to warn them," I said to Deborah. "Even with the way they're treating me… I can't just say nothing. Saving those lives is more important than anything else."

I'm not sure where you're going with this, Lorelei, but I'll follow your lead however you need me to.

I raised my voice to carry out into the hall. "Hey! Can anyone hear me? There's something I need to tell you about the fearmancers and why they're here. People's lives are on the line!"

They didn't come running this time. It was at least a full minute before the sharp-eyed woman returned to the room, the muscular guy flanking her. She frowned at me. "What are you talking about? What's this you want to tell us now?"

I wet my lips with nervousness I didn't need to fake. "I —I know what the other fearmancers have come here to do. And if you don't reach out to them and come to some kind of agreement, a whole bunch of joymancers will die tomorrow."

The guy stiffened. "That sounds like a threat."

As if he was anyone to talk. I managed not to roll my eyes. "I'm not saying it that way. The whole reason I came here in the first place was to try to negotiate a way for both sides to be happy without a lot of violence. I was just hoping we could have that discussion on more equal footing. But if this is how it's got to be… I still have to speak up."

The woman lifted her chin. "All right. Speak up then. What's going on?"

My stomach knotted as I forced myself to cross the line I'd avoided so far. "We found out that my birth mother is still alive. A team of fearmancers has come here to take her back. They know where you're holding her, and as soon as additional forces arrive tomorrow evening, they're going to make their assault."

Both of the joymancers had gone rigid during my announcement. Deborah tucked herself closer to my leg with an anxious shiver. I couldn't tell whether she approved of me taking this step or not... I wasn't even sure if *I* approved of the outcome yet.

"Where are they?" the woman demanded. "If we can get the jump on them—"

I shook my head vehemently. I had to trust that Lillian and the other blacksuits knew how to cover their tracks well enough that it wouldn't be easy for the joymancers to find our hotel. "No. That's the exact opposite of what I'm here for. I don't want *them* dying either. I don't want anyone dying, even if apparently that's a difficult concept for everyone else to swallow."

The man's mouth twisted. "You can't expect us to just stand back and wait for them to come at us."

"I don't," I said emphatically. "I want you to negotiate, like I said. You've held the Bloodstone baron for seventeen years without giving her any chance to see her family or her people... I have no idea what you've done to her during that time, but it can't have been anything but agonizing for her. Whatever you would accuse her of, you've punished her plenty. If you give her up to the fearmancers without a fight, then there won't be a fight."

The woman sputtered. "We can't just *give up*. Lord knows what they'll think they can get away with next."

"That's why it's a negotiation. You can make demands in return. Form a magical contract to ensure the fearmancers will keep to their side. Isn't there anything that'd be more useful to you than keeping my mother captive even longer?"

"Or we could just bolster our defenses and fend them off," the guy said.

I fixed him with my hardest stare. "It won't work. I've seen their plans—I know the inside information they've been able to gather about the building. They've got every possibility covered. Do you really think they'd go in to rescue one of their barons without being completely ready to shatter any protections you try to put in place? As long as she's in that place, they're going to get her out. It's only a matter of how many people die along the way."

From the woman's sickly expression, I'd convinced her. The guy I found harder to read, but he certainly didn't look happy.

"We don't negotiate with fearmancers," he bit out, and stalked through the doorway with a gesture for the woman to follow him. I watched them go, trying to ignore my own queasiness.

I'd planted the first seed with that warning and tying it to the specific building. Now I had to give them as much of a nudge as I could in the right direction without being obvious about it.

I gave them a couple of minutes to get back to their previous spot. After what I'd just said, surely they'd still have someone monitoring me. When the timing felt right, I sucked in a breath as if in dismay.

It worked well enough that Deborah believed it. *What's wrong?* she asked.

"I forgot," I said, keeping my voice low but not so quiet it'd be inaudible to someone listening closely. "I might have ruined everything. The blacksuits did say there'd be a window when they can't have anyone directly watching the place... They were talking about having to leave just magical sensors in place to let them know if anything changed in the area—around noon, maybe it was? Shit. If the joymancers realize no one's around to stop them, they could move my mother someplace we don't know about, put even heavier deflective spells around her, and we might never find her again."

Please, let the joymancers be listening. Please let them think what an amazing idea that was. My whole plan hinged on them taking the bait.

There was no way I could know if they had, though. Deborah scrambled up onto my lap and curled up next to my elbow. *Whatever you're doing, I hope it works. Do you still want to break out of here?*

"Yes," I said, figuring this was safe enough to say out loud. "As soon as possible."

Let's give them a little while to calm down, and then I'll see what I can do.

The events I'd intended to set in motion might work even if I was stuck in here the whole time... but they'd work a whole lot better if I could give Lillian a heads up in advance. I closed my eyes and sent up a silent prayer that an opening would present itself before we ran out of time.

CHAPTER TWENTY-THREE

Declan

M y brother's hair had gotten shaggier since I'd last seen him. The black strands fell across his eyes as he huffed his way up the last flight of stairs in the junior residences. He had a big duffel bag slung across his back as well as a suitcase in one hand; I was lugging a second suitcase behind him.

"You know, one of the benefits of having home just a couple hours away instead of on the other side of an ocean is you don't have to bring every possession you own to school with you," I pointed out wryly. "If you realize you forgot something you need, it's not that hard to get it."

"Now you tell me." Noah shot an amused smile my way. "I like to live in comfort. Maybe the French spoiled me."

They had, but not in the way he was thinking. After

doing his first two years of schooling abroad, he had no idea what life was going to be like at Blood U.

We got a taste just walking into his assigned dorm room. All of his dormmates had come out into the common room in anticipation of his arrival. Most newcomers wouldn't get quite that eager a welcome, but the young fearmancers wanted to check out the kid who was second in line for the Ashgrave barony.

"Ashgrave!" said a guy I knew my brother had hung out with occasionally before their school years. His family's property wasn't far from ours. "Finally decided we were good enough for you, huh?"

Noah laughed. "Maybe I heard you all weren't coping so well without me and decided I should take pity on you."

It was normal seventeen-year-old-style ribbing... except it also wasn't. The other guys chuckled and tossed out a few remarks as we carried Noah's things to his corner room, but I caught the anticipation in certain expressions, the analytical consideration of some of those gazes.

Noah wasn't used to looking out for himself the way I was. No one in Paris had given a crap about his last name —it'd conferred no special standing there. Here...

Some of his dormmates would be looking to suck up to him for whatever benefits that might grant them in future, sure, and that wasn't so bad. But others would see his presence as an opportunity to make a show of their own dominance. The jockeying for power between the regular fearmancers was bad enough. If someone saw an opening to prove themselves stronger than a potential scion? They'd jump on that chance the second they thought they could get away with it.

As Rory had discovered in uncomfortable clarity during her first month on campus, before everyone had found out just how strong she'd be once she got a handle on her powers.

Even without the older barons scheming away, Noah couldn't exactly consider himself safe here. Which was partly why I'd offered to help him get settled in. He strode right into his room, but I stopped on the threshold and glanced back at the other juniors. A *stern* glance, with all the authority I'd learned to convey over the years and a clear message: anyone who messed with my little brother was messing with a soon-to-be baron as well.

The guy who'd greeted him first just nodded, so maybe he'd be okay. A couple of the others averted their eyes with nervousness that might have had a little guilt mixed in. As long as the nervousness won out over their desire to make a name for themselves at my brother's expense, we were good.

Noah was puttering around his room with his luggage unopened on his bed, peering into the wardrobe, running his hands over the desk.

"A bit of a letdown after Paris?" I asked.

He gave me a crooked grin. "Actually, my room at the school there was half this size. The bed too. But it did have a more interesting view. There's a hell of a lot more to do when you're on the edge of a big city."

"You'll have lots of chances to visit New York," I said. "Even if that's not quite as impressive as Paris either. The

European mages don't seem to have quite as much to worry about from opposing factions as we do." From what I understood, while both fearmancers and joymancers existed elsewhere, the tensions between them ran higher here than anywhere else. Lucky us. It was a lot easier to stay hidden on an isolated property where you could lay down as many strong wards as you wanted without interfering with the Nary population.

Noah didn't look particularly bothered, though. He dug into his bags and started hanging up clothes in the wardrobe. I let him figure all that out, sitting down at the desk while he worked. When he'd put away everything he appeared to feel he needed to for the moment, he dropped down on the side of the bed.

"My internal clock has gotten totally out of whack," he said. "I was exhausted when I got home this afternoon, so I took a nap, and now that it's actually dark out, the last thing I want to do is sleep."

"Why don't I show you around the rest of campus while I'm free to?" I suggested.

"That sounds good." He stretched out his legs, which might have gotten even longer than mine in the last couple years while he'd been mostly away at school, and stood up again.

Night had fully settled in outside, the fields dark beyond the ring of lights along the buildings that surrounded the green. I pointed out the hall that bore our family name where he'd find the library and my own dorm, and the Tower where he'd have his classes starting tomorrow. Then we wandered on toward the Stormhurst

Building and the lake beyond it. A few stars twinkled overhead amid streaks of cloud. The grass rustled under our feet.

"Have you given any thought to taking a familiar?" I asked. "I know you put it off because of the hassle with international travel."

Noah nodded. "I'm still debating what kind of animal would be the best fit. I know what a long commitment it is."

Especially since the magical bond allowed the animals to live quite a bit longer than they might have otherwise. I was glad to hear him approaching the idea with that much foresight. "Well, if you want to talk through the possibilities, you can always call on me. You can call on me for anything you need advice on, really. I'm only going to be at the school a few more months, so you might as well make use of that benefit while you can."

Noah looked sideways at me with a lift of one eyebrow. "I *have* been at a magical school for more than two years now, even if it's not this one. I think I'll get along all right without having to turn to my big brother for support too often."

"It's not that I don't think you'll adapt just fine," I said quickly. I wasn't looking to squash his confidence. Just to… moderate it. "The social and political dynamics here are going to be a lot more complicated, that's all. In ways you're not totally used to." Maybe I shouldn't have sent him off to broaden his horizons when that meant he wasn't fully prepared for the situation here. A few months wasn't much time for him to get used to the change in his peers' attitudes.

A spring came into Noah's step. "Hey, I'm looking forward to diving into all that political stuff. Maybe I'm not scion, but I should be able to lend a hand here and there. It's going to be boring as hell sitting in the background the whole time."

I shot him a stern look. "You won't be sitting in the background. You'll figure out what you'd be happiest doing with your life, and then you'll go do that. You just need to be careful along the way. Because of your position, people will try to use you—by seeking favors and by looking for ways to undermine you to make themselves look stronger. It sucks, but you have to stay wary and on guard much more than you'd ever have had to be in Paris."

"Let them bring it on, then." Noah clapped his hands together. "That's what goes with being an Ashgrave. I can handle it."

How could he know that when he'd never had to before? I grappled for the right words to get across just how seriously he needed to take my warning.

"It's more than just the others students. There are pressures and conflicts from all over…" I glanced around, distrusting the darkness. Sound could travel far across open ground. I motioned him over to the woods so we could at least have a little shelter before we went into any more detail.

"I've heard you and Dad talking," Noah said as he followed me over. "I know there's a lot of stress and all. Obviously way more on you than there'll be on me. But you don't need to coddle me. I've got to get used to it sometime, right?"

"It's not that simple. You have to understand…"

I trailed off until we'd walked several paces through the brush. With a couple of quick castings, I confirmed no one else was nearby and then formed a bubble of silence around us so anyone who happened to come our way wouldn't overhear us. Then I turned to my brother, touching his arm to emphasize how much I needed his attention.

"I'm not just talking people giving you a hard time or twisting your arm for an inside edge or whatever. I haven't wanted to discuss a lot of this with you because, well, the more you know, the more of a target it makes you. And I didn't want you having to carry those worries around when you were younger. But you need to know enough to protect yourself."

"What are you talking about, Declan?" Noah asked.

I exhaled in a rush. "The pressures we face are a matter of life and death. All right? Do you know Dad had to fend off at least three attempts to murder me before I came into my magic? Attempts that couldn't be traced to the source, because otherwise we could have called for an arrest, but it's been obvious from the start that Aunt Ambrosia would happily see both you and me dead when that gives her a clear path to the barony."

Noah blinked at me. "You're saying Aunt Ambrosia tried to *kill* you?"

"Arranged scenarios that would have been deadly if not interrupted, would be more accurate." I made a face.

"And that's just one example. A lot of mages want the kind of authority we have, or want to stop us from exercising that authority, or simply see us as an access point to getting at the barony as a whole... The Ashgraves don't have the reputation for being particularly ruthless, so people are more inclined to try us than, say, a Nightwood or a Stormhurst."

"Fuck." Noah kicked at a fallen twig. But when he looked up at me, I didn't see the caution I'd been trying to inspire in his face. No, his expression was all fierce conviction. In a way, it reminded me of Rory. "We can't let them get away with that crap. They *won't* get away with shit like that now that you've got me here. The two of us together, especially as I get even better with my magic— we'll be a real force to be reckoned with. I'll have *your* back, whenever you need me."

"Hey. I want to keep you out of the dangerous side of politics as much as I can." I raised my hand to his shoulder and squeezed it. "*I'm* going to be baron. It's my job to protect my family. And part of that is preparing you for what you can expect here."

Noah shook his head. "No way. I told you I don't want to just sit back. Maybe I'm younger, but I've got three magical strengths just like you do. I'll catch up. I *want* to help. I want to fight whoever we need to fight, however we need to fight them. Don't shut me out."

I didn't think I really could now that he was here. He'd be tied to me regardless of how much distance I attempted to maintain between our roles. But his determination sent a twinge of uneasiness through me all the same.

Why did he have to be so enthusiastic about getting involved? It'd have been a hell of a lot easier to keep him safe if he'd taken the warning as I'd meant it rather than as a call to battle.

"I won't," I said. "You're going to do the Ashgrave name proud too. But for now, take it slow, pay close attention to everyone around you, and watch before you leap. We won't win fights we stumble into by accident."

"Got it." He acknowledged the point with a jerk of his head, immediately followed by a yawn he couldn't clap his hand over fast enough. "Okay, I think I might be ready to hit the sack now. Point me in the direction of Killbrook Hall, and I'll be good."

I walked him partway across the field to where he could see the building easily, and he gave me a mock salute before continuing on his way. A weight settled onto my gut as I watched him go.

Maybe there hadn't been any good way to warn him. Maybe this was just how it had to be. At least I'd given it my best shot.

The thought of fraught baron politics brought my hand to my phone as I headed to my own dorm. I hadn't seen Connar or Baron Stormhurst since I'd run into the other scion a few hours ago. It wasn't as if *he* couldn't generally handle himself or his mother had any reasons to come down hard on him right now, but still… I knew he didn't enjoy his parents' company either.

Hey, I texted him. *How's it going? Up for a night cap in the scion lounge?* If his mother had been hassling him about Rory again, we could strategize together.

The reply took long enough that I was already getting concerned when it finally popped up.

Headed out of town for the next day or two. Private shifter tournament came up that looked like a good opportunity. We'll catch up after!

There wasn't anything about the wording that sounded specifically un-Connar like. I frowned at the message anyway. Multiple times in the past, I'd heard the Stormhurst scion complaining about the fact that his mentor kept pushing him toward various tournaments. He'd been clearly relieved whenever Malcolm had used some sway to justify his refusal.

Perhaps his mother had proposed attending this one, and he'd simply thought it was better not to argue with her about this on top of existing tensions. Still, the explanation didn't totally sit right.

I considered my phone for a few seconds longer and then shoved it into my pocket with a sigh. Unfortunately, no matter how I felt about it, there wasn't anything much I could do in the absence of any evidence of wrongdoing. I'd just have to wait to check in with him whenever he made it back to campus. Hopefully sooner rather than later.

CHAPTER TWENTY-FOUR

Rory

None of the joymancers came back for quite a while. I didn't have much sense of time without any points of reference—if there was a window in the room beyond, it was out of my view from the closet. It had to be night by now. How late into it, I had no idea. My mind was getting groggy from jetlag and lack of sleep, but the constant sense of the minutes slipping away before the fearmancers noticed my absence kept me semi-alert with a buzz of anxiety.

Deborah couldn't have had any more idea of time passing than I did, but after a while she apparently decided it was safe for her to make a move. *I'm going to take a look around and see what our best course of action is*, she told me. *I'll try to be back quickly. Hold strong as well as you can.*

Despite those last words, a pang of deeper fear shot through my gut as she darted out of the room. She could decide to throw in her lot with the other joymancers after all. Or she could simply get caught and I'd lose even that one small ally. There was nothing I could do while I was shut up in this makeshift prison.

I got up and walked around the chair a few times to stretch my legs. Then I fiddled with the cuffs around my wrists some more to see if maybe I could work them loose after all. My activities didn't bring any joymancer observers, so I was going to guess they didn't have a visual on me, only some way of listening in.

I wasn't much of a threat without my magic, after all. Along with restraining me, they must have drained me. When I'd been cuffed by the fearmancers, I'd still been able to feel the magic coursing through me; I just hadn't been able to shift it. Right now, that spot behind my collarbone felt utterly empty. Even if I got out of the cuffs, I'd have to frighten someone before I'd have any power.

The minutes slid by even more unnervingly while Deborah was gone. I strained my ears for any sound of a commotion from the hall, but nothing reached me.

The joymancers might have bespelled the room to muffle sounds from beyond anyway. They wouldn't want me listening in on their conversations.

Finally, my familiar's little white body scurried back through the doorway. Relief washed through me. Something glinted on her fur and below her head. When she scrambled onto my lap, I saw with a flicker of surprise that she was carrying my dragon charm on its silver chain.

I know this isn't going to help you in here, she said, *but I*

*saw the opportunity, and I didn't think you'd want to leave
without it if you didn't have to.*

My heart swelled. I wasn't sure it was a good idea to
thank her out loud, but I nodded in a way I hoped showed
my gratitude.

*I'm going to go back for the key to your cuffs. I should be
able to get the chance to grab it, but I'm not sure how long
we'll have before they notice. You'll need to be ready to get out
of here as fast as you can once you have them.*

I looked down at my wrists. Did she really think it'd
be that simple? I opened my mouth, fumbled with the
words to ask her in a way that wouldn't alert my jailors,
and motioned to the doorway in front of me. "I can't," I
said quietly, hoping she'd understand.

*I've no doubt you have enough power to break any spells
they have holding you here once you have the chance to use it.
At the moment, the way to the front door is clear. Once the
cuffs are off, you can tear down the barrier and simply run.*

It took me several more seconds to express the
problem with that. "I don't have anything," I settled on,
my spirits sinking. If her whole plan depended on my
magic, we were shit out of luck.

*Oh, sweetheart. They've only tricked you. The energies
joymancers work with are too different from yours to really
diffuse the magic you have inside you. They haven't forced you
into any castings, so whatever power you had when you
arrived here, it's still in you. The cuffs only dull your
awareness of it so you can't sense it to cast with it. It's the best
strategy they have for unexpected conflicts like this.*

My magic was still there? I reached toward it the way I

would have if I'd been going to cast, but all I touched was the same emptiness as before.

But if she was telling the truth, I wasn't empty. I was only numb. We could do this, as long as I didn't give the game away too soon.

I nodded again, my pulse thudding faster. That response must have satisfied my familiar. *One more thing you should watch out for*, she added. *I saw them casting on you while you were knocked out. From what I've been able to overhear, I believe they placed some sort of tracking spell on one of the buttons on your shirt. You'll want to get rid of those as soon as you can once you're out of here.*

I glanced down at my shirt. It had just two small metal buttons, more decorative than functional, just below the center of the collar. And one of those could have led the joymancers right to our hotel. My stomach listed queasily.

"Thank you," I said.

Deborah nuzzled my arm. *You're a good one, Lorelei. Don't let the joymancers* or *the other fearmancers change that.* Then she leapt down to the floor again and raced away.

I sat up straighter in the chair, my thoughts whirling as I worked through my hopeful escape. Deborah would come with the keys. Where were the keyholes on the cuffs? Turning my wrists, I made out the shape of the spots on the undersides and confirmed I could reach one side with the opposite hand if I stretched. It'd be tough to get a good fit, but I should be able to manage it. It wasn't as if Deborah could handle that part for me.

Once they were off, according to her, I should be able to feel my magic again. I could already picture how I'd smash through the barrier in front of me. There might be others—in the doorway to the room outside, or in the hall… I'd need to send a stream of magic ahead of me to detect any obstacles.

A straight run down the hallway to the door was simple enough. I'd probably be running *past* at least one room where the joymancers were working, though. No matter how quietly I did my casting, they might catch on and come rushing to stop me before I'd even made it to the hall.

It didn't sound as if the additional people they'd been waiting for had arrived yet, though. With my magic, I should be able to push past them. I could… shove them into one of the other rooms and put a magical lock on them. It wouldn't have to be all that complex to hold them for the short time it'd take me to make it to the door.

Once I was outside, I'd just keep running. I couldn't forget to grab my phone from the shrubs at the front of the yard—it'd be ten times as hard getting away without that. I could snap both the buttons off my shirt just to be safe and call an Uber to someplace several blocks away, dash over to meet it, and be on my way back to Sacramento before the joymancers had a chance to figure out which way I'd gone.

There were a lot of uncertainties in that plan still, but it was the best I was likely to get. I rehearsed the sequence in my mind over and over: unlock the cuffs, break the barrier, shove aside the joymancers, dash out the door, grab the phone, snap off the buttons, and run like hell.

After a few iterations, it started to feel as solid as if I'd already done it.

I shifted forward on the chair so I could tilt at a better angle for reaching the cuffs. My mouth had gone dry. I swallowed thickly, waiting and waiting with the pounding of my heart—

—and Deborah bolted through the doorway with a tiny keyring clamped in her jaws.

I had no time to think, no time to do anything except launch straight into the chain of actions I'd been picturing. She scrambled up to my knee, I snatched the key from her, and my wrists strained against the metal binding.

In the first second, the tiny object almost slipped from my fingers. I pinched it tighter and maneuvered it into the first hole.

As soon as that cuff had snapped off, a trembling sensation rose up behind my sternum. My spirits leapt, but I couldn't afford to rejoice just yet. I rammed the key into the opposite cuff and snapped that off my arm too.

The sense of my magic flooded me, as potent and heady as it'd always been—maybe even more so now that I'd had to go hours without feeling it at all. Deborah clambered up to my shoulder as I sprang to my feet. I set the cuffs gently on the seat so they didn't make a sound to bring the joymancers running already and turned my focus to the barrier in front of me.

The words I'd chosen rolled off my tongue with a harsh breath I hoped would disguise them. I trained my attention on the center of the doorway and sent a blade of magic ramming straight into it like an axe.

The conjured wall resounded with an echo of the impact that quivered over my skin, but the barrier held steady. I clenched my hands and spat out the spell again more forcefully, over and over in swift repetitions.

On the fifth, the barrier shattered. I flung myself through the doorway and the room beyond, intent on the hall. With one more murmured casting, I sent a thread of magic winding ahead of me.

They'd sealed the doorway to the hall too. I bit back a curse. As I opened my mouth to attack it, a distant yell reached my ears.

They'd already noticed something was wrong. Shit.

I battered the new barrier with the same casting, not quite as cautious this time. Speed mattered more than secrecy now. With a jerk of my hand, the third impact split that wall of magic down the middle. I wrenched the tremoring energy aside and bolted through it.

Three figures were already charging down the hall toward me—the man and woman who'd questioned me, and the guy who'd originally let me in. I barreled on toward them, Deborah's claws pinching my skin through my shirt as she clung to me.

Before my jailors could cast anything at me, I'd already spoken the spells I'd planned. A wave of energy smacked them to the side and clamped their mouths shut at the same time. I sent them tumbling through an open doorway in a heap.

"Shut," I called out as I hurtled past, and the door banged closed with magical force.

Maybe someday they'd remember that I hadn't killed them to make this escape, hadn't even hurt them, even though the lethal approach might have given me more certainty of success.

The entrance lay straight ahead of me. I sprinted for it with a burst of exhilaration fueled by my apparent victory. There were magical locks on the door, but I could break those too. And then I'd be home free.

I'd just tossed a disabling spell at the locks when someone sprang from another doorway and sent a spell crashing into me.

I'd assumed all the joymancers around had already been rushing to contain my escape. A potentially fatal miscalculation. I slammed into the wall with a jolt of pain through my shoulder.

The man who'd battered me whipped up his hands as his lips moved to cast another spell. The breath had been knocked from my lungs. I sucked in air, fumbling for some sort of defense and knowing I didn't have time to pull it off.

My lips were just parting when a small white shape launched itself from my shoulder.

Deborah threw herself into the blaze of the joymancer's spell just as it shot from his hands. "No!" I choked out.

The bolt of fire hit her body and consumed it in an instant. A tearing sensation radiated through my body from throat to belly. A tiny fall of ash pattered to the floor.

Panic, anger, and agony collided in my mind. I managed to sputter a casting word in a ragged voice. The energy I whipped out knocked my attacker off his feet and pinned him to the floor. I hesitated for a few precious seconds, searching the ground as if my familiar could somehow emerge, as if the wrenching of our broken bond could be a lie.

"Deborah?" I croaked.

There was nothing. And with each moment I delayed, I might make her sacrifice meaningless.

With my eyes swimming with tears, I staggered around and lunged the last few steps to the door.

The cooling air in the darkness outside prickled across the wetness streaking down my cheeks. Every step sent fresh shockwaves of pain through my chest. I swayed on the sidewalk and managed to grab my phone on autopilot. Swallowing sobs, I fled into the night.

CHAPTER TWENTY-FIVE

Rory

As the car slowed outside the hotel, I came out of my daze of pain and grief with a brief jolt of panic. I hadn't thought through making my return.

"Keep going, to the end of the block," I said quickly.

The driver obliged without any visible reaction. I clambered out into the glow of the streetlamps that turned the night sky above hazy.

An alley around the corner gave me enough shelter to cast the reflective illusion. My magic stirred sluggishly across the ache that ran through my chest. I had to mutter the words more forcefully before the effect stuck in place.

My legs trembled. I leaned back against the rough brick wall and touched the indents on my shirt where I'd remembered to tear off the buttons just in time, a few blocks from meeting my driver. I'd checked myself over as well as I could in my muddled state afterward and hadn't caught any hint of joymancer magic on me. I should be safe from *them*, at least.

After several seconds, I pushed myself onward toward the hotel.

It was a good thing I'd taken precautions. One of the blacksuits was standing in the shadows near the hotel entrance. I stopped in my tracks when I saw her and stayed in place until another patron came up to the doors. I managed to slip in behind him and passed another blacksuit on the way to the elevators. Thankfully, the man I was following was heading there too. I just waited until he'd gotten off before I pushed the button for my floor.

A fresh wave of physical loss hit me as I stepped out of the elevator. A wrenching sensation tore up from my gut to my ribs. I stumbled and nearly fell on the floor, which would have been just great for keeping a low profile. The thump probably would have brought half the blacksuits out of their rooms in an instant.

I managed to catch my balance, but as I crouched there, catching my breath, the thought of going back to my room and trying to sleep through this horror made my stomach twist even tighter. I was still going to be a total mess in the morning—maybe even worse than I was now. I had to get it together. And I wasn't sure I could do that on my own.

I straightened up and took a few wobbly steps down the hall. The door to room 1506 was right across from mine. I hesitated there, wavering in indecision, but really, what other reasonable option did I have?

Malcolm had said he'd come so someone here would

have my back. I might as well give him the chance to show whether he could really make good on that promise, right?

I didn't knock, just murmured, "Open," to the lock. The tiny light over the keycard slot flashed green with a faint click of the deadbolt. I eased the door forward and slipped into the dark room. With a wave of my hand and a quick word, I dispelled the reflective illusion.

It was *very* dark—it was well past midnight now, and Malcolm had pulled the blackout curtain fully closed. I stood there in the room's foyer for a moment, letting my eyes adjust to the faint glow of the clock on the bedside table. I couldn't make out more than the vague shape of Malcolm lying between the covers, but the rhythmic rasp of his breath told me he was asleep.

Until I moved toward him, anyway. Maybe it was a shift in the air or the whisper of my feet against the floor, but I'd only made it halfway across the room before his form twitched and his breath stuttered. His hand swiped over his face. "Rory?"

Abruptly, I felt both insanely out of place and desperate for guidance. My throat choked up, making my words stumble. "I—I'm sorry. I needed... to talk to someone, and I thought—"

He was already sitting up, reaching for the bedside lamp at the same time. A flick of the switch flooded us both with stark light. He took one look at my face, and concern with an edge of protective fury flashed across his. "What the hell happened? Has someone been hassling you?"

He started to get out of the bed, the sheet falling away

from his bare chest, which I'd have appreciated more if I'd had any capacity for desire at the moment. My knees wobbled under me. I sank down onto the far end of his bed, and Malcolm halted, sitting up at the edge just a couple feet from me. He extended his arm tentatively to take my hand.

Something about the gentle contact cracked the composure I'd been holding onto so tightly since I'd fled the Conclave headquarters. The tears I'd managed to suppress by the time the Uber had shown up burst out in a torrent, along with a sob I couldn't quite swallow. I gulped for air and tried to get control of myself again, but the anguish that filled my chest wouldn't relent.

"Hey," Malcolm said, sounding startled. He shifted closer and tugged me to him at the same time. "Hey. Whatever the hell it is, we'll make it right. Do you need me to get Ravenguard?"

I shook my head emphatically as I tipped it to his shoulder. His arms squeezed around me. "No," I managed to force out. "No. If she found out, she'd kill me."

"Found out what? Talk to me, Rory. You can't pretend it's no big deal."

I wiped at my eyes, doing my best to avoid leaking tears all over him. I hadn't really thought through how much of the story I'd have to tell him for the important parts to make sense. But it was a little late to backtrack. "You'll probably want to kill me too," I mumbled.

Despite everything, his voice turned dry. "Even when I thought you were a shit-stirring traitor who was out to deliberately undermine me and the other scions, I never wanted to kill you. I think you're safe."

A ragged laugh sputtered out of me. I took a few more breaths, slower and steadier, until the choking feeling eased back. Malcolm kept his arms around me, his head tipped by mine so his chin rested against my temple with a comforting firmness.

"The whole reason I insisted on coming with the blacksuits to California is I'm afraid of what they're going to do to get my mother back," I said. "They're so... *furious*, knowing the joymancers have kept her captive all this time, knowing they failed to realize... Of course there's going to be a fight; of course it'd be pretty much impossible to get her back without anyone dying, but I'd just like it to be fewer people rather than more."

Malcolm sighed. "No surprises there. That's about the most Rory sentiment I've ever heard. So, what does that have to do with this?"

"Well, I— We did the locating ceremony yesterday afternoon, and as soon as the blacksuits had the location narrowed down, they went into assault mode. Lillian has these conducting weapons that can basically mow down all kinds of people with the same spell. It was obvious they don't care who gets hurt along the way, even bystanders. I couldn't stand the thought of just sitting around while they planned some kind of slaughter. So I..." I swallowed hard. "I snuck out and went to the joymancer's headquarters."

"*What?*" Malcolm's head jerked up, his body stiffening against mine.

"I thought I might be able to arrange some kind of negotiation," I blurted out. "That they might listen to me because I grew up more like a joymancer than a fearmancer. I just—I had to try. But they wouldn't listen at all. They refused to even consider believing that I honestly wanted to help. They treated *me* like a prisoner. I had to get out and get back here. But to do that…"

My throat closed up again. That was the worst part. I'd gone out there hoping to save lives. Instead I'd cost Deborah hers. If I'd just stayed here, if I'd stayed out of it, she never would have had to protect me like that.

Malcolm was still tense, but he'd relaxed a little with my explanation. "To do that?" he prompted quietly.

"I brought my familiar with me," I said. "When I was escaping, one of the joymancers came at me at a moment where I wasn't totally prepared. I couldn't defend myself in time. She jumped right into the spell he was aiming at me so it'd hit her instead of me. It *killed* her."

The tears spilled over again. Malcolm inhaled sharply and hugged me tighter. "Fuck," he muttered. "No wonder you're messed up. Those bastards."

"It's my fault." My voice came out watery. "I brought her there. I came up with the plan in the first place." I couldn't even tell him the worst of it—that I'd lost more than just a bonded pet, that my mouse had held the spirit of a human being as well. I pressed my hand to the center of my chest. "It *hurts*. The broken bond."

"Of course it does. God. I haven't had to experience that yet myself, but I know—it's always hard, and it's hardest if you lose your familiar in some violent way instead of a peaceful passing on."

Malcolm stroked his hand over my hair, and I found myself tucking my face closer to the crook of his neck. The lingering sharp aquatic scent of his usual cologne filled my nose.

"It *isn't* your fault," he went on in a firm tone. "You still had some faith in those assholes. You gave them the benefit of the doubt, because that's who you are. And I know—I know your parents, at least, weren't awful people. If you could have negotiated something, it'd have been better for our side too. It's not likely we'd get through a full assault without losing any of our own in the process. But the joymancers screwed you over. You can't blame anyone but them."

I wished the situation were as simple as he made it sound. "I don't know how well I'll be able to hold it together tomorrow around the blacksuits... Is there anything I can do that'll make coping easier?"

"I don't know. From what I've heard, you basically have to wait the pain out. Like any other wound, it'll start to heal on its own. But it should get better with time. If you're still feeling awful tomorrow, you can always make up some excuse like that you're nervous about what the joymancers will have done to your mother."

"Yeah." I was going to have to explain the plan I'd set in motion to Lillian somehow or other too. Dread crept in beneath the pain, but I gritted my teeth against it. I could worry about that when the time came.

Malcolm's fingers skimmed over my hair again. "Are

you sure you're safe? There's no way the joymancers could have tracked you after you left?"

I shook my head. "I took care of that. At least, as far as I know, I did." Although, while I couldn't believe Deborah had misled me, that didn't mean she couldn't have been mistaken. And I hadn't exactly been in the clearest mindset when I'd scanned myself.

I scooted back a little. "You could check me over for any sign of a spell just to be sure. My necklace should have illusion magic on it, but otherwise there shouldn't be any."

His gaze swept over me as he murmured a few casting words under his breath. After a minute, to my relief, he nodded. "You're good. The bastards aren't finding you that way."

"Good." I edged closer to Malcolm again, and he tucked his arm around my waist.

He paused before saying anything else. "I'm glad you came to me. I mean, I know you'd probably rather have had one of the other scions to turn to, but I want you to be able to rely on me now too. So... thank you for considering me-in-person to be at least a slightly better option than just texting the other guys."

There was a certain amount of self-deprecation in his voice, but not enough to stop the sentiment from feeling genuine. And maybe he was right. Maybe I'd have hesitated less about asking for help if it'd been Declan or Jude or Connar here with me. But... they weren't, and he was.

"You're the one who insisted on being here," I said. "That means something." I paused. "I know I gave you a hard time about going behind my back to arrange it, but I'm glad you came. I'd have felt really alone right now otherwise."

"Well, you're definitely not that. I wish I could do more. What do you need from me?"

He asked the question so easily and simply that I suspected I could have made just about any request and he'd have done his best to fulfill it. With that offer, the past fell away, and I had no doubts at all about whether I could trust the guy next to me in every capacity.

But there wasn't much I really wanted at the moment anyway, not that I could have. I wanted Deborah to still be alive. I wanted the pain inside to numb. I wasn't going to get either of those things. Other than that... I was exhausted. And the thought of wobbling back to my room and collapsing onto the bed where I'd spoken with my familiar just hours ago turned the ache inside into a dagger.

"I need to sleep," I said. "And if it's okay with you, I'd rather not be alone for that either."

Malcolm touched my cheek and leaned in to press a quick kiss to my forehead. I half expected another joke about having me in his bed, but apparently he took my pain a lot more seriously than he had his own.

"What's mine is yours," he said. "There's plenty of room. Take as much as you want."

He slid over to the other side of the bed, leaving space for me to crawl under the covers next to him. Maybe I should have felt awkward about this intimacy after how complicated things had been between us, but it seemed perfectly natural, if perhaps only because of how freaking tired I was. I lay my head down on the pillow and rested my hand on his arm. At that encouragement, he eased himself over so he could touch my waist in a partial embrace.

The warmth of his body spread beneath the covers to envelope me. I closed my eyes. The tearing sensation of the broken bond radiated through me, but my fatigue was even more potent. In just a few minutes, sleep pulled me under.

CHAPTER TWENTY-SIX

Malcolm

I'd never really shared a bed with anyone before. Even after five years mostly sleeping in my dorm, my reflexes from the many years in my parents' houses before then kept me on high alert to any nearby disturbance.

It took me over an hour to get back to sleep with Rory beside me, every slight stirring of her body jolting me back into full awareness. Even after I adjusted enough to drift off, I jerked awake a few more times throughout the night without being completely certain why.

I'd just have to continue adjusting until I could really relax. Because I wanted to do this again, as many times as she'd come to me.

I woke up one last time at her shifting onto her back. A hint of sunlight peeked past the blackout curtain, and the clock read just past seven. I could tell I wasn't getting any more sleep. That was fine. In the moment, I couldn't think of any better way to spend my time than gazing at the girl dozing next to me.

Rory's dark hair was strewn across the pillow in adorable disarray. Her face had softened as she slept, shedding most of the anguish that had tensed her features last night. Her brow had stayed slightly knit, though, and one hand had clenched against the center of her chest where I suspected the severed familiar bond must be hurting the most. A faint ache pulsed in the same spot on my body after spending nearly twenty-four hours across the country from my own familiar.

I should have felt annoyed that she'd gone running to the joymancers—that she'd still had enough trust in them to think it was worth the attempt. Maybe I was, a little. But at the same time, I was sharply aware of the fact that if the Bloodstone scion hadn't kept such an open mind, hadn't been willing to give even those who'd mistreated her the benefit of the doubt... there was no way she'd have been lying in my bed right now. So it was hard to resent that part of who she was.

The fact that she was here at all seemed like even more of a miracle than when she'd appeared in my bedroom while I'd been enduring my father's punishment. I didn't dare touch her in case I woke her from the rest she obviously needed—and because some part of me was ridiculously afraid she'd somehow vanish as if she'd never been here.

I'd earned this trust. I'd proven that I could make up for past mistakes. I had to keep reminding myself of that, because I suspected it was going to take a while before *I* fully believed I deserved her forgiveness.

I hadn't moved, but Rory emerged back into consciousness with a yawn and a few blinks. She stared up at the ceiling with a frown that looked puzzled for a second before it tightened with renewed pain. Her throat worked as she turned toward me.

"Good morning," I said, even though it didn't appear to be all that good as far as she was concerned. "How're you doing?"

She swiped her hair back from her eyes and rubbed her mouth. "Still feel like shit. Both emotionally and physically. But it's probably not quite as intense as last night." She dragged in a breath and let it out equally slowly. Her deep blue eyes brightened a little as she gazed back at me. "Thank you for talking me through it. For letting me stay."

"You're welcome, although that didn't exactly require Herculean effort," I said. What did was refraining from pulling her to me and finding out whether I could kiss some of the discomfort off her beautiful face.

To my great joy, I didn't have to. Rory scooted closer under the covers, setting her hand on the side of my bare abdomen with an instant flare of heat, and tipped her head to bring her mouth to mine.

My body lit up from crown to soles, desire unfurling through me in a flood. I cupped her jaw and kissed her back the way I'd wished I could the other time she'd lain in a bed next to me. Her fingers traced over my abs, and I had to tamp down on a groan. My cock was half hard already.

Rory looped her other arm around my neck, bringing our bodies flush against each other. She devoured my mouth, her tongue searing hot, her hips straining against mine, and I was hard as marble now. It took all my self-control not to roll on top of her and strip every scrap of clothing off her right then. She was giving every indication of *wanting* me to do that… but I couldn't shake the image of her pained frown, of her hand clenched against her chest.

Rory caressed the planes of my torso again, her fingers like licks of flame, and I did groan then. For a second I couldn't focus on anything but the heat of her exactly the way I'd wanted her for so long.

But I was a goddamned scion. I wasn't going to be ruled by my dick.

I forced myself to pull back, even though every inch of my skin was humming at attention and clamoring for more, and grazed my fingers over Rory's cheek. "What are you trying to do here, Bloodstone?"

She grimaced, possibly at both the question and my use of her last name. "I don't think I'm being all that subtle about it. Isn't this what *you* wanted to do?"

My proposition yesterday. And yes, I had wanted to get her moaning in my bed, but that'd been before everything she'd gone through last night.

"I remember that," I said with a raise of my eyebrows. "I want to know why you're up for it all of a sudden."

She ducked her head with a flush in her cheeks that

brought out both my protective instinct and a fresh stirring of lust. "I want to feel something other than… this," she said, pressing her hand to that spot on her chest. "Just for a little while. Something that doesn't hurt."

Ah. I'd been afraid of that. A Nightwood—or *this* Nightwood, anyway—had higher standards.

Keeping a tight rein on my desires, I touched her chin to nudge her gaze to meet mine. "I get it, Rory," I said. "But when we do this the first time, I want it to be because you can't stand the thought of *not* having sex with me right this instant. No reasons beyond what's happening between you and me. No room for doubts or regrets afterward. All right?"

The color in her cheeks darkened with obvious embarrassment. "I'm sorry. I didn't mean—"

She started to scoot away from me, but I caught her by the waist, still holding her gaze. "Hey. I'm not upset. And if we'd already crossed that bridge before, I'd happily have taken the opportunity to escape everything else for a while."

Rory's shirt had ridden up while we'd made out. My fingers rested against bare skin. My cock twitched, and fuck, I wasn't *that* much of a saint. A little indulgence wouldn't be so terrible.

I eased those fingers farther up, under her shirt, watching her expression. "There are still other ways I could help distract you. If you'd like."

Rory wet her lips. The gleam came back into her eyes. As my hand reached her breast, she arched into my caress. I stroked my thumb over the curve of her flesh, pressing harder over the nipple, and her breath caught. Then she dove in to kiss me again.

The kissing made it harder for me to keep my head, but I left a little distance between our bodies, fondling one breast and then the other until Rory made a mewling, desperate sound against my mouth that just about made me come without any contact down below.

As much as I wanted to taste the rest of her, I didn't think pushing things that far would be wise for sticking to my principles. So I focused on kissing her mouth with all the heat and desire I had in me while trailing my hand down to the waist of her pants.

She inhaled shakily as I dipped my fingers under the fabric. I teased them over the thin layer of her panties and then under that as well.

She was so fucking wet I could have exploded. I flicked my thumb over her clit, and her head tipped back from mine with a ragged sound. It turned out I got to have the heir of Bloodstone moaning in bed with me after all.

I might not have spread around my talents quite as far as Jude did, but I'd had a fling here and there over the years when I'd been sure the girl and I were on the same page—that her interest wasn't just some ploy to hook a scion. And I'd aimed to keep my reputation between the sheets as solid as everywhere else. I definitely didn't deserve *this* girl if I couldn't make her come.

I worked her over gently at first, noting every hitch of breath, every flutter of her eyelids, every hungry sound. It didn't take long to see exactly where to apply pressure and how deep to slip my fingers inside her to start her trembling.

Her hand wrapped around my arm, clutching me but not in any attempt to stop me. Just holding on as I took her on this ride. My cock couldn't have been harder, and my groin was aching seeing her losing herself to pleasure, but I could survive that. This, right now, was all about her.

I pressed a little harder, plunged inside her a little faster, and a cry broke from her throat. I couldn't say I'd ever felt anything like the blaze of triumph that washed through me as her body clenched around my fingers and then sagged with its release.

She reached for my face and drew me to her for a kiss that was still just as hot, but this time long and lingering.

"Did that do the trick?" I murmured by her ear afterward.

"Exactly what I needed," she said with a smile that was almost giddy, but the corners of it had already started to tighten again. What I'd offered really had been only a distraction. The deeper pain couldn't be fingered or fucked away.

My cock was still hard as anything. I was trying to figure out how exactly I was going to manage to peel myself away from her when a knock sounded from beyond the hotel room door. Not on *my* door, though. It had to be someone at the room across from mine.

Rory tensed. With the second knock, a muffled voice carried to us. "Miss Bloodstone?"

The blacksuits must have come to call on her.

She sat up, straightening her clothes, combing her

fingers through her hair, and froze. "It wouldn't be good if they realize I was in here with you, would it? Someone would tell your father."

There were plenty of practical reasons to keep our more intimate involvement a secret. In the first instant, I wanted to give all of them the finger and announce my adoration to the world. Only the first instant, though. The last thing Rory needed was for me to make my father even *more* intent on breaking her down.

I hopped out of bed and grabbed a pair of slacks out of my suitcase. "No problem. Tell them you just came over to join me for a room service breakfast. Friendliness between scions. No one likes to eat alone."

I picked up the hotel phone and managed to place a hasty order to support that story while fumbling into a shirt. Rory jerked the bedcovers straight and gave herself a once-over in the mirror before heading for the door. She appeared to have accepted my idea, but she didn't look all that much less tense. I guessed she couldn't be looking forward to hearing whatever updates the blacksuits had for her.

She glanced over at me as she reached for the handle, confirming I'd pulled myself together. I ambled over to the little table in the corner and dropped into one of the chairs as if we'd just been sitting there talking while we waited for our order. Rory exhaled audibly and tugged open the door.

The blacksuits in the hall had been in the middle of calling out to her again. The voice cut off as the speaker must have seen her.

"Sorry," Rory said, with a determined calm that only made me admire her more. "I was just going to have breakfast with Malcolm. It seemed silly to eat by myself. Has something happened with my mother—or the joymancers?"

The voice that answered her wasn't the one that'd been calling at her door. "We haven't taken any definitive action since we last spoke," the woman said, equally calmly. "I wanted to make sure you've recovered from the final ceremony without any issues, and I thought you'd like an update on our plans."

That was Lillian Ravenguard. Rory's mother's best friend. My father's co-conspirator. My jaw clenched, any lingering arousal from my interlude with Rory deflating.

"Of course," Rory said. "There's actually something I need to discuss with you about those plans. Why don't you come in here, since Malcolm might as well hear this too, and we're waiting on that breakfast anyway?"

What was she planning on pitching to the blacksuits now? By her own admission, her attempt at initiating a negotiation with the joymancers had failed. She hadn't mentioned any other schemes. I gave her a quick curious glance as she turned toward me, but I had to pull my expression into a mask of casual benevolence at the sight of Ravenguard and the two blacksuit lackeys who'd come with her.

The woman took in my pose at the table, the unrumpled bed, and Rory as if evaluating her story. She might wonder if we'd actually been together for more than breakfast, but I thought we'd composed ourselves pretty well. Rory had changed for her nighttime adventures, so she was even in a different outfit from what the blacksuits would have seen her in before. No walk-of-shame yesterday's-clothing giveaway there.

Rory sat down at the table across from me, and Ravenguard pulled out the chair from the desk to face her. The other two blacksuits stayed standing, like sentries, by the door.

"We know exactly which building your mother is in now, and we've identified the magical defenses around it," Ravenguard said. "There has been increased joymancer activity around the place this morning, but nothing we can't overcome. They may have caught a hint of our presence."

Rory's mouth twitched as if she'd resisted biting her lip. She kept her voice steady. "That's actually what I wanted to talk to you about. Through my... past associations with the joymancers, I've been able to find out some of their intentions. They're going to move my mother to a different location today, before they expect your attack."

Ravenguard stared at her. *I* stared at her. How had she managed to determine that—and where the hell was she going with it?

"How would you know this?" the blacksuit demanded.

Rory gave her a weary smile. "I remembered an old friend of my parents. It occurred to me that I could use them to sway the joymancers' strategy. I made sure I didn't give away anything that wouldn't work in our favor."

"You should have consulted with me first."

"It was a brief opportunity. There wasn't time. I'm sorry about that." Rory nodded toward the door. "I assume you'll want to get a new plan in motion as quickly as possible. The joymancers think our forces will have pulled back around noon, leaving only spells to monitor the building. That's when they'll make a run for it. But that also makes it the perfect chance for you to strike. You wait until they're on the move, and then you can ambush them somewhere out in the open while they're less able to defend themselves. That's better for us, isn't it?"

"I still don't—" Ravenguard cut herself off, obviously feeling the urgency Rory had mentioned and seeing the Bloodstone scion meant what she said. She let out a breath in a huff. "We'll have to be much more restrained in our use of magic outside in the middle of the day."

Ah, that explained everything. Even captured and with her and her familiar's lives at risk, Rory had managed to spin the situation toward the less-fatal outcome she'd wanted, even if she hadn't pulled off quite the coupe she'd hoped for.

"So will the joymancers," she said. "We still have the element of surprise on our side. I have every faith that the blacksuits can use this opportunity to their advantage and bring my mother back uninjured."

In that moment, with her posture straight and her voice forceful and clear, she was every inch a baron already. And that was exactly how to play a woman like Ravenguard. The blacksuit looked as if she'd swallowed another complaint. She squared her shoulders. "Of course we will. Even sooner than expected. I'd better make sure we have everything in place. Thank you for that unexpected information—which I would like to hear more about later."

As she got up, Rory's gaze lifted to follow her. "There's one more thing," she said in the same commanding tone. "I want to be there."

Ravenguard halted. "At the attack? Rory, we've talked about this. I can't put you in that kind of danger—"

"I know," Rory said. "That's not what I mean. I just want to be close enough to see what happens. It's *my* mother you're rescuing. I want to be able to go to her the first second she's out of the fray."

Ravenguard's mouth flattened. I could tell she wanted to argue, but Rory's framing hadn't made it easy. That didn't mean she wouldn't, though.

I couldn't contribute much to the plan Rory had somehow orchestrated, but I could at least help this request of hers along. It was obviously a hell of a lot more important to her than anything I'd been able to offer so far.

"I'll stay with her," I said before the blacksuit could find the right argument. "I'll make sure she stays well back from the fighting—and be an extra line of defense if it comes our way."

I gave Ravenguard a meaningful look as if to say she should know I'd have her—and my father's—best interests at heart. Ravenguard wavered for a moment and then nodded.

"All right," she said. "We'll see what we can do. Have your breakfast and be prepared to move out at our call."

CHAPTER TWENTY-SEVEN

Rory

The dry wind blew across the ten-story rooftop and tugged at my hair, which I'd pulled back into a ponytail a few minutes ago to keep it out of my face. The sun shone bright, bringing out the chemical scent of the asphalt surface I was standing on—and glancing off the many pedestrians on the street below. I hoped their presence meant the mages on the verge of battle would exercise greater caution, not that there'd be even more Nary casualties.

I couldn't make out any of the blacksuits stationed around this strip of the city, but that was the whole point. Even my lookout spot here was hidden by an illusion and a persuasive repulsing spell. Surprise *had* given us the upper hand. Lillian's people had been able to catch enough of the joymancers' preparations around the city to figure out what general route they were planning on using to transport my mother. Now we were just waiting for them to arrive for the ambush.

Lillian had been carrying that conductive weapon when I'd last seen her. Dear Lord, let her decide not to use it in the midst of all the bystanders below.

Malcolm shifted against the concrete wall he was leaning against. "They are taking their time."

I shot him a look with my arms crossed over my chest. "No one asked you to play babysitter. You could be relaxing back at the hotel if you wanted."

He shot me the cocky grin I was starting to appreciate in ways I'd never have expected to a couple months ago. "Someone's got to keep an eye on you. I don't think your blacksuit keeper would have agreed to you being even this close on your own." He shook his head in amusement. "You do like being a wild card, don't you?"

"Sorry if I don't have much taste for bloodshed," I muttered, but he was right about Lillian. I wasn't really sure I'd have been able to insist on tagging along even to this extent without company, and she wouldn't have wanted to spare any of the blacksuits for that purpose.

"Just one more thing to work on," Malcolm said with a wink, but his expression softened a moment later. "You seem to be holding up all right."

That was a subtle question about my well-being, which I couldn't blame him for after the state I'd come to him in last night. And the way I'd thrown myself at him this morning.

My face warmed a little remembering, but that heat wasn't all embarrassment. If I'd had any doubts about the

Nightwood scion's capacity for generosity, they were gone now. Although that'd only made me more curious about what it'd be like to finally fulfill the desires we'd both been keeping reined in for so long now.

Between my fears about the impending attack and the pain of the inner wound that was healing only slowly, it wasn't so hard to avoid temptation at this particular moment. I appreciated his concern, though. I sucked in a breath, feeling out the achingly empty space between my lungs.

"I'm not sure how much it's gotten better and how much I've just gotten used to coping," I said. "But the loss isn't overwhelming anymore, at least."

He nodded. "You've had to cope with worse. Fortunately or unfortunately, it gets easier with practice."

A comment he could obviously make from personal experience, considering how nonchalant he'd been about his father's retaliation after my hearing.

"I'm hoping to avoid much more practice at losing familiars." And friends. The knowledge that Deborah was completely gone hit me all over again. I inhaled slowly to push back the wave of grief.

I had nothing and no one from my old life left except for the single glass charm hanging around my neck, which I'd almost lost too. And I couldn't even claim the fearmancers had stolen it all away. The joymancers hadn't been able to see me as anything other than an enemy, and because of that, they'd destroyed the one real connection I had to any joymancers other than my parents.

I'd already decided that I was going to make the best

of my life with the fearmancers and push for the changes I wanted to see from within the pentacle of scions and then barons, but my experience here had basically ensured that was the only viable option. I didn't trust the Conclave any more than I did Malcolm's father.

My senses caught a faint shifting of magic. Something was happening. I leaned against the wall overlooking the street, searching the road and the sidewalks. Malcolm turned to follow my gaze.

I knew the vehicle from the eerie shimmer that clung to it, an impression that would have been unperceivable to the Naries nearby. It was a heavy gray truck that looked like the sort of thing a bank might use to transport stacks of cash. I guessed that said something about how valuable the joymancers considered my mother to be.

The truck was flanked ahead and behind by sedans that might also have held joymancers. I couldn't tell how many might be in the windowless back of the truck. The Conclave would have assigned as many mages as they could to protecting their precious cargo. But they couldn't disguise it completely, not when they needed to drive alongside Nary traffic. Their stealthy transport could be ruined in an instant if a regular driver took a turn into a truck they'd turned invisible.

I braced myself, watching for the first move of the attack. Lillian wouldn't want the blacksuits to reveal their magic too openly... but she also wouldn't risk losing my mother again. There were dozens of Naries around in their cars and walking by. If my gambit meant *more* of them got hurt, there'd be no one else I could displace that guilt onto.

"It's already started," Malcolm remarked at the same moment that I realized it too. The pedestrians I'd been watching had either sped up or meandered off down side-streets, slowly clearing the sidewalks near the truck. The cars behind the second sedan turned off in other directions too. No new cars were approaching in the opposing lane.

The blacksuits were surreptitiously clearing the path as much as they could—so they could get away with more magic than they could have risked otherwise, but I appreciated the side benefit.

That thought had just passed through my head when the truck lurched with the bang of a misfiring engine. The cars ahead of the first sedan sped away as if in the grips of a sudden panic—which they probably were.

Magic flashed back and forth across the street like blazing streaks of sunlight. My fingers had curled tight around the lip of the wall, the rough concrete digging into my skin. I flinched at a strangled cry that carried from one of the sedans.

Something crashed in an alley nearby, followed by a pained cough. The truck rocked on its wheels, but it didn't budge from where it'd been stopped. With a hiss sharp enough that I could hear it even from so high above, the tires sagged flat.

Several figures spilled out of the back of the truck, slamming its doors behind them. Their arms were already waving and their mouths moving with castings.

Flickers of movement caught my eyes along the street

around them where the concealed blacksuits were returning fire. With one brutal blast, half of the joymancers flew backward off their feet, their heads smashing into the side of the building behind them.

I'd known we couldn't avoid bloodshed completely, but the sight still made my stomach turn. My gaze jerked from one end of the street to the other as I tried to track the battle.

The remaining joymancers, including a bunch that had scrambled out of the sedans, were forming a ring around the truck. And maybe a magical shield, from the way the next few spells hurled their way burst into a glimmering shower before reaching them.

How long until they struck back—or until the fearmancers smashed through their wall and their bodies? Lillian and the others had to be at least a little cautious to avoid hurting my mother in the truck.

More spells slammed back and forth across the street. The impact reverberated through the air up to where Malcolm and I stood. I shuddered with it—and my gaze latched onto a cluster of figures approaching on the side-street across from us.

My first instinct was defensive, seeing them as potential attackers. But it only took a second to realize they were anything but. It was a group of young teens, presumably drawn by the unexpected sounds, creeping closer to take a peek at the action.

A peek that could get them killed.

"Shit," I murmured. Malcolm's head snapped around to see what I was responding to. I shot him a quick glance and decided I didn't care whether he approved of what I was about to do or not.

I'd wanted to be here so I could take some responsibility for the events I'd set in motion. Now was my chance to do just that.

Without any more hesitation, I turned my attention back toward the lurking teenagers and summoned a strong waft of magic from my chest. "*You don't want to be here,*" I said with the punch of a persuasive casting. "*There's something back the way you came from that you really need to check out.*"

Even though they couldn't hear me, the power of the spell hit them firmly. A few of them started backpedaling, and then they all turned and hurried away down the alley.

I got to relax for about five seconds before Malcolm muttered a curse. He'd turned to peer along the side of the building we were perched on. I hurried over to join him.

Four figures were stalking along the alley there with a ripple of magic around them that told me these weren't innocent passersby. They weren't blacksuits either, which meant they were reinforcements from the joymancers. Sneaking over to try to get the jump on our forces.

I didn't think Lillian would have left her people's flanks unprotected. The blacksuits could probably take this group on—by smashing their skulls in like they'd done to the other joymancers. My stomach clenched at the thought.

"I'm dealing with those," I said.

Malcolm paused as if he was considering arguing, but

then his lips curled into a defiant smile. "Just say the word, and I'll be right there with you."

"We just… get them out of the way until the fighting's over." I could even use the same basic trick I had in the Conclave headquarters. The joymancers were just coming up on an open dumpster. I nodded to it and raised my hands. "Contain them."

With another heave of my magic, I cast out my spell with the simplest words that came to me. "Up and in!" Malcolm barked out a casting word of his own at the same time.

As I flicked my wrists, the bodies of the four joymancers whipped off the ground and plunged into the heap of garbage bags.

"Shut and stay," I said with all the force I could summon. The dumpster's lid thumped closed. It rattled with the impact of spells from within, and Malcolm snapped out another casting word. After that, the lid didn't budge.

"I don't know how long that'll hold," he said, turning to me. "But I think it should be long enough to get us through the fight."

A sudden pang ran through me. The Nightwood scion had been here for me at my hearing and every time I'd needed him since, but I still hadn't totally believed he'd ever buy into all of my values rather than dismissing some of them as weakness. He'd just saved four joymancers from their probable deaths, because I'd said that was what I wanted to do.

"Thank you," I said. The words didn't feel like enough.

"Maybe I'm losing my taste for bloodshed too," he said with a smirk, and brushed a stray strand of hair back from my cheek. The graze of his fingertips set my heart thumping even faster. "Don't let anyone tell you that you can't run things your way, Glinda—not even me. You're fucking perfect the way you are."

There was nothing but affection now in the nickname he'd used to say so disdainfully. I swallowed hard.

A shattering sound split the air. I spun back toward the front of the building.

Glass littered the pavement beneath the broken windows on the sedans and the cab of the truck. The bodies of the ring of joymancers lay sprawled amid the glinting shards. Several blacksuits were stalking across the road to the truck.

My legs itched to run down the stairs to be there when they opened it, but I knew the battle wasn't likely to be over yet. That suspicion was borne out moments later when the truck's doors clanged open.

Joymancers leapt out, flinging spells in every direction. A few of the blacksuits stumbled and fell, their bodies sagging, burnt or bleeding. But this had obviously been the joymancers' last-ditch effort. Lillian and the other blacksuits shouted castings, and the remaining attackers crumpled. She shoved one body aside with her foot and climbed into the truck.

I couldn't wait for more confirmation than that. I dashed for the stairwell, Malcolm loping along behind me, and hustled down the steps as fast as my feet would carry me. My breath was raw in my throat by the time I reached the ground floor, but I ran right out into the street.

Lillian and one of the other blacksuits were just carrying a limp form out of the truck, cradled between them. Even though I had no memory of ever meeting the woman they held, my pulse stuttered. I sprinted over to them. My lungs constricted at the sight of her pale, gaunt face before I could force out any sound.

"Mom?" I said automatically.

Her eyes didn't open. Her whole body was gaunt, almost skeletal—had the joymancers been *starving* her?

Horror flooded me, but Lillian's voice jarred me out of my shock. "We've got to get her out of here before the Conclave sends more of their people. Come on—to the cars. She'll be all right after our doctors have had a chance to see to her properly."

My mouth opened and closed. Malcolm set a hand on my shoulder. "Let's get her home," he said.

I let him nudge me toward the vehicles the blacksuits had parked farther down the street, but I couldn't tear my eyes from the woman.

We'd rescued her—my birth mother, the Bloodstone baron. But she barely looked as if she'd survived.

CHAPTER TWENTY-EIGHT

Rory

The blacksuits' medical wing looked a lot like I'd expect a hospital to—white walls, narrow cots, bright light fixtures overhead—and it had the same sharply clean smell. The only difference was the eerie quiet. My shoes squeaked faintly every time I shifted my weight on the polished floor. So I held still, gazing down at my mother where she lay on the cot they'd given her.

"Has she come to at all yet?" I asked Lillian, who'd joined me for my visit.

My mother's self-proclaimed best friend shook her head, but she didn't look concerned. "Our doctors have your mother in a state of deep magical sedation to give her mind and body time to recover," she said. "It shouldn't need to last more than another day or two, and then she'll be better prepared to continue that recovery consciously. It's a common technique, nothing to worry about."

The woman on the bed did appear to be a lot healthier than she'd seemed when I'd first seen Lillian carrying her from the joymancers' truck. Her skin had warmed from sallow beige to pale peachy pink. The angles of her face and limbs didn't look quite so skeletally sharp, so I guessed the fearmancer doctors were giving her some kind of nutrition. Someone had washed and brushed her hair, too, so the mingled silver and dark brown strands lay sleekly on her pillow.

She'd changed from the woman in the photograph and videos—aged and worn down—but I recognized her, both with my eyes and on that bone-deep level with which my spirit had responded to hers when the blacksuits had used me to stretch their magic across the country.

I tried to imagine what it'd be like if she woke up right now and gazed into my eyes. What expression would she make? What would she say to me? My mind stalled trying to generate a plausible answer.

What I knew of her was a big mess of contradictions. The woman who'd lovingly cradled my infant self in her bed; the woman who'd chummed up with Baron Nightwood. The woman whose fury I'd tasted across thousands of miles; the woman who slept so peacefully in front of me. She could be all of those things. I wouldn't know which elements guided her the most until she was conscious again.

"Is there anything I can do?" I asked, even though I didn't see how there could be. I'd asked the same question when we'd made it back to New York last night, and the blacksuits hadn't suggested anything then either. I had to check all the same.

As expected, Lillian only grimaced. "You've already done so much to bring her back. Catch up on your schoolwork, reconnect with your friends, and I'll let you know as soon as the doctors have settled on an awakening time. I know she'll want to see you as soon as she's up."

"Of course," I said. The thought sent a quiver through me that was equal parts excitement and nerves.

I was her daughter, her only heir. That would count for something. And if she wanted things from me I wasn't willing to give, I didn't have to answer to her. A week ago, I'd been nearly baron myself. I had to remember that.

The inner pep talk didn't stop the anxiety from chasing me through the drive back to campus. The niggling sensation took up residence in my chest next to the dulling but still unshakeable ache of Deborah's death.

Before I'd left to visit my mother, I'd already gone around to check with my professors about the classes I'd missed while I was in California. I didn't have any classes today until later in the afternoon. After I'd parked the family Lexus—which maybe would go back to being my mother's once she was up to driving again?—I wandered over to the scion lounge.

The guys had been waiting for me. Well, most of them, anyway. They were standing around the pool table, Malcolm waving his cue as he talked like a king with his scepter, Jude jumping in with an elaborate flourish and a joking remark that set the other two laughing, Declan shaking his head at the two of them with a small but fond smile.

When I'd talked to them briefly after we'd gotten in from California, Declan had said something about Connar leaving on a short trip for some magic-related event. The Stormhurst scion hadn't replied to my text this morning, so I guessed it was keeping him pretty busy. I wasn't going to let myself add that to my expansive list of worries just yet.

The guys all looked up when I came in. Jude tossed his pool cue on the table and leapt to my side with a flash of a grin, tucking his arm around my waist as if to remind the other guys—or maybe himself—that he could. I leaned into him as Declan and Malcolm ambled over. Declan appeared unfazed by the show of affection. Malcolm's jaw tightened slightly, but if he was struggling with any possessive urges, he mastered them before they got ahold of his tongue.

The Ashgrave scion grasped my other hand briefly with a reassuring squeeze. "How is she?" he asked.

"They still have her sedated," I said. "I think she looks better, but it's hard to tell when she's unconscious. Lillian said they'd be waking her up in a day or two."

"And then we find out what the joymancers put Baron Bloodstone through all this time," Malcolm said grimly.

We didn't need much more than what we'd already seen to confirm they'd treated her awfully. I made a face in answer.

"We'll find out what kind of a baron she's going to be from here on, too," Declan put in. From his grave expression as he considered me, I suspected he could guess what sort of worries might be plaguing me.

"If she's ready to be baron again after all," Jude said, and kissed my cheek. "Maybe she'll save us all a lot of trouble and pass the title on to Rory right now."

Malcolm guffawed. "I don't think there's much chance of that. When in the history of the pentacle has any baron capable of making the choice decided to hand over their power early?"

"Not in any instance the records I've looked at covered," Declan admitted.

Jude shrugged. "No harm in having hopes. But hey, we've taken on three barons and come out on top. One more shouldn't be so bad."

"She *is* my mother," I said. "She might be on our—my —side."

Even I couldn't say that with total confidence. A solemn silence filled the room for a few seconds with the knowledge of how little parentage had benefitted the heirs of the other three older barons.

"Well, I suppose we'll just have to wait and see," Malcolm said. "Jude's right. Even if she becomes part of the problem rather than solving it, we can handle it. *This* pentacle couldn't be more solid."

He smiled at me with a quiet warmth that felt like a secret between us. Something in my chest fluttered. Was it possible I could find myself loving him too—loving all of the guys I was meant to rule beside?

All the guys I'd have to give up before we got to that

point, except for Jude. Who still wasn't ready to tell the others that.

Malcolm's phone buzzed with a notification. He pulled it out, and his expression warmed in a different way. "Connar's finally back. He can tell us how the hell he let himself get roped into whatever exactly he's been off doing." He lowered the phone. "He's just coming over from the parking lot. Let's give him a break and meet him halfway. If he actually did let himself get caught up in some tournament, he's probably in a shitty mood."

Maybe I could help with that. I followed the guys up the stairs from the Ashgrave Hall basement with a spring in my step at the thought of seeing the last of my lovers again. It might have been selfish, but something was missing without him—just as it would have been without Jude or Declan... or even Malcolm now, if I was being honest.

Whatever my mother's return might mean for us, I prayed with every ounce of my being that we were ready for it.

ABOUT THE AUTHOR

Eva Chase lives in Canada with her family. She loves stories both swoony and supernatural, and strong women and the men who appreciate them. Along with the Royals of Villain Academy series, she is the author of the Moriarty's Men series, the Looking Glass Curse trilogy, the Their Dark Valkyrie series, the Witch's Consorts series, the Dragon Shifter's Mates series, the Demons of Fame Romance series, the Legends Reborn trilogy, and the Alpha Project Psychic Romance series.

Connect with Eva online:
www.evachase.com
eva@evachase.com